THE BRIDGE TO FAE REALM

RON COLLINS

SKYFOX
PUBLISHING
Fantasy

Skyfox Publishing

ISBN-10: 1-946176-49-4
ISBN-13: 978-1-946176-49-3

For the downtrodden, the dark, and the untethered

The Delivery

It was August and sunny, which, in Savannah, means humidity only slightly more comfortable than having a swampy towel jammed down your throat.

The piece of shit delivery van shuddered as Jon pulled to the curb in front of the Oglethorpe Club, a three-story building at the corner of Gaston and Bull. The van was *not* one of the new units, not one with a super-clean engine and padded seats, or that didn't rattle your spine every time you hit the goddamned accelerator. His boss, Lannie the dick, was set in his ways, and nothing short of Mother Teresa coming out of … retirement … would make him give one of those machines to a guy like Jon, who Lannie saw as a complete loser and a massive drain on society.

It didn't matter that Jon worked his ass off, or that he was the most reliable guy on the staff. It didn't matter that he'd been clean for six months, or that his case worker gave him nothing but outstanding marks. And it most definitely didn't matter that he had *always* hit every deadline he was given in his other "job," which consisted of writing reviews and music news from the clubs around town.

Life wasn't like that.

Instead, Jon got #26: this brown box of crap he thought of as Beelzebub on wheels, a unit that reeked of diesel fuel and old French fries, took three tons of force to engage the parking brake, and had a broken spring at the base of its seat.

Not that he was bitching.

At twenty-two years old, and as a guy who hadn't been able to stand still long enough to graduate high school, better yet college, Jonathan Hale had already given up on the idea that he was anything special as far as the "real world" went. The mere fact that he had a job at all right now made him a lucky man.

That was all right though. If Jon knew one thing by now, it was that all learning didn't come from books. He knew how things were. He would find his own goddamned way, despite Lannie the dick.

He threw the clutch and took #26 out of gear.

The van's engine dropped to a hard idle as he leaned on the parking brake, then reached back to the staging shelf where his ten-thousandth package of the day sat, daring him to drop it.

He glanced out the window then.

… across the way.

… into Forsyth Park.

The girl was not exactly what he would call stunning.

Not cute.

Not fine, beautiful, gorgeous, smokin', amazing, drop-dead, or any one of the hundred other descriptions Jon would have used to convey something about the appearance of a young woman he found … attractive.

She was, however, so interesting he couldn't take his eyes off her.

She was his age, maybe younger, all elbows and knees sitting at the base of a massive tree in shade made strong by the thick patch of sycamore and elm that grew in the park.

She wore tan leggings that disappeared into brown boots that rose to the middle of her spindly calves. Her sleeveless top was as dark as the leaves above her. It exposed the sharpness of her shoulders and a cascading tattoo of something viney that fell down her arm to disappear into the crook of her elbow. She was Latina, he thought. Or maybe light-skinned African. Her face was thin and smooth, and a little longer than normal. Her cheekbones were sharp like a model's, but out of whack in a way that made her lips appear poutier than she probably liked. Her long hair was a colored mass that gleamed with the entire spectrum of green—yes, green—but vibrant and bold in a way that totally worked for her. It was formed in a cloudlike mass that was both dense and fine, maybe even permed given how a few strands waved in the breeze.

Very underground chic.

She was reading a real book, too. A trade paperback with a title Jon couldn't make out. And she was actually smoking, drawing languidly on a thin brown cigarette that released faint clouds of greenish smoke to waft away in that same almost-there breeze that made her hair wave.

Her fingers danced as they turned the page.

When he looked at her, Jon got the feeling that something was going to happen.

She looked up.

Her eyes were deep wells of brown surrounded by white. She drew her dark lips back into a crooked smile. It was a startling expression, but also a familiar one, almost confrontational in its directness. It said she had been waiting for him.

He smiled back at her.

Then a horn blared from somewhere behind him, and he jumped so hard he nearly broke his hand against the big-assed steering wheel in front of him.

"Goddamnit!" he yelled as he shook the pain out.

He glanced at the side mirror.

It was a trolley bus stopped behind him.

He had left plenty of space to get by, but the idiot behind the wheel just sat there with his over-large glasses pushed up on the bridge of his piggy little nose, and leaned on the horn again and again until Jon wanted to jump the hell out of the van and go punch the guy. It was a goddamned Ghost bus, too, three-quarters stuffed with the usual collection of gawk-eyed stooges who had paid their 15 bucks apiece for the privilege of lapping up a forty-five-minute, piece-of-crap spiel about the antebellum south, the elegance of the

Confederate lifestyle, and, of course, the ghost walks. The whole damned ride was just one big, ass-clenching advertisement for *another* set of tours that started a half hour after the sun went down and carried on until there wasn't a dollar left to squeeze from the wallets of any tourist gullible enough to fall for it.

Jon wedged the box onto his hip and slipped out the door.

He began to sweat the minute the sun hit his uniform.

A car rushed by as he clutched the box to his hip. The package wasn't heavy, but its bulk made Jon feel klutzy. #26's valves clicked and clacked in the heat, and T-shirt-clad families chatted with the straw-hatted locals who were out doing their workaday shopping. An old VW was stopped at the intersection, waiting to turn right, its engine also blatting away.

Jon motioned back to the trolley driver.

"Go on around!" he yelled.

The idiot made a big-assed show of twisting the wheel.

Somehow, Jon managed to keep from rolling his eyes until he made it to the top of the concrete stairs and past the doorway. "Asshole," he gave himself permission to utter once he was inside.

Progress, he thought. *It comes in such small packages.*

The Oglethorpe was a traditional Gentlemen's Club, meaning it was a place of stature rather than one of the more hedonistic ventures others might think of when they heard the term "Gentlemen's Club." He stepped into the air-conditioned lobby, feeling more than a little out of place, and left the package with the receptionist—waiting for several very long seconds while she read the fine print before signing the receipt.

As he waited, he thought about the girl.

He should talk to her. What would he say? Maybe he could ask if she wanted to go to a club over the weekend. She gave the vibe, anyway. When he returned to the sidewalk, the Ghost Tour bus was rolling further on down the road.

But the girl was gone.

"Crap," he said.

He felt like the wind had been kicked out of him as he watched the bus turn onto Whitaker Street and leave behind a trail of heat waves. In the distance, behind those waves, Jon caught sight of a musclebound man struggling to walk a pair of dogs.

The animals were big and black, the man big and white.

Jon sighed and pushed a flop of hair off his forehead.

He looked to where the girl had been.

The need to see her pulled at him, which wasn't anything goddamned new. Even before the drugs, Jon had felt things more than he thought them. His friends gave him shit because he always followed his heart more than his brains.

But there was something about her.

She was different.

He just didn't know how.

As he peered at the tree, Jon saw the girl's book stuck at the roots —yes, the book. No doubt about it.

Anxious, he scanned the area as #26 sat idling in the midday sun.

Would anyone rat him out if he took a break?

It wouldn't take much time and, like always, he was ahead of schedule.

That's all that should matter, right? Make sure every customer gets their shit when they expect to get it, and the world can keep right on going around and around. As long as he kept to his schedule, the worst that should happen was that Lannie the dick would make him ride #26 for another week, which he could pretty much guarantee anyway. And if some asshole *did* eventually call the office, and Lannie decided to use that as an excuse to give him an extra ration of shit, well, so be it. He'd been in worse fixes.

In the end, he saw only one logical choice.

Jon crossed over the street and through the grassy lawn before entering the shade and coming to the base of the tree. It was a sycamore big enough around that even his abnormally long arm span wouldn't make it halfway.

Forsyth was the biggest of Savannah's parks, and, as such, it had a hundred of these things, maybe more, big and black, with twisted branches that rattled in the wind and made them look like something out of *Labyrinth* had mated up with something from *The Game of Thrones*.

The shade made it cool here.

Leaves rustled, and the shade made it almost as dark as evening time.

The faint hint of the girl's cigarette lingered behind, a spicy essence, unfamiliar but pleasant as it hung in the heavy air alongside the presence of living wood.

The voices of young kids echoed from the playground, their high-pitched lilt mixing with the splatter of water that came from the old, rounded fountain that sat in the clearing maybe fifty feet away.

He had come here before, mostly to lean up against that fountain while he listened to new demos, something that helped him focus when he was struggling. A lot about life sucked when you were living it alone, and the fountain had always seemed to help.

He put his hand on the tree. Its bark was firm and rough.

Jon looked to where the girl had been sitting.

There. The book. Stuck behind a big-assed root.

It wasn't a paperback.

Instead, it was more like an old scrapbook, sheets of thick parchment bound with leathery straps. Like the tree, the book was old. Words were scrawled in faded brown ink across its front, but in a language he couldn't read.

He picked it up, and the hair on his wrists tingled.

Perplexed, he put the book to his nose.

It smelled … wonderful … like a mix of cinnamon and brown sugar.

It was a deep aroma, edged with a sense of excitement. It came with the exact feeling he got when he walked into a shitty hole-in-the-wall dive and heard a fresh band for the first time—a group with the real stuff—maybe before even *they* knew they were something special. It made him want to write.

Who was this girl? he thought.

The throaty sound of dogs growling broke his thoughts.

They were on the walkway—the same pair of beasts he had

seen earlier, big and black, lean and hard, pulling with feverish intent against the leather harness being held onto by a muscular man wearing dark glasses and a skintight T-shirt.

The man's lips were drawn in a line that said they were here for a reason.

"What's up, dude?" Jon said, gripping the book harder.

The dogs kept coming, maybe ten paces off now.

"Get the hell away," Jon yelled, cocking his arm back to defend himself, and holding the book like it was a rolled-up newspaper.

Pages slid open.

Symbols snaked across the parchment, and a thin drumbeat rose up, oddly in sync with the rhythm of the #26's idling engine. He smelled the book stronger now. Leaves gusted into a crescendo, and a curtain of green smoke rose to swirl around him.

The dogs' breath was a furnace. Their snarling drove harder against the normalcy of the day. The display of their teeth locked into his brain.

He raised an arm to protect himself, and as he stepped back his foot *thunked* against a root.

The book flew from his grasp.

He twisted, trying to grab it back, but instead, his stomach turned as he fell into a slow, wavering drop.

Backward toward the tree.

Backward … *into* … the tree … through the air and through the bark, through things he couldn't have named even if a damned *Jeopardy* champion whispered them into his ear. He fell through phloem, through cambium, down and down through what seemed like never-ending rings of sapwood before he hit the firm heart at the core of the tree.

The drumming became a flow here.

The smell of sugar soaked through him, and the essence of corded fiber stretched from his fingers and his toes through the ground and up to the sky.

Where am I? Jon thought as he crashed down.

Where the hell am I?

Into the Woods

A sharp root hit his thigh as he landed.

The ground was dry and prickly. He spit a mouthful of grit as he raised his head up.

It was nighttime.

Pitch black until his eyes adjusted.

"Get up," a voice said. "We have to get out of here."

He was in a forest, but definitely *not* Forsyth Park.

The girl knelt beside him, her green hair framing her face. Moonlight etched the slim contours of her body, and the tattoos down her shoulders flared with violet and lavender. Her gaze was firm. From this close he saw the girl's upper and lower lips were both pierced at their centers, and that she wore a thin dagger hitched to a twine belt that circled her waist.

"It's you," he said, feeling like an idiot the moment the words left his mouth. "Where are we?"

She drove one of her knees hard into his hip. "I said to get your ass up."

The girl stood, towering over him.

Jon glanced at the tree he had fallen into, or out of.

A looming surface hung there, gleaming with internal light like a magical pane of glass or a mystical mirror filled with the soundless images of the dogs from the park as they slavered and pawed against its other side.

Cold air prickled his skin.

The woods crackled with sounds he couldn't separate out—low, hissing sizzles and pops that reminded him of something from an old vinyl record. The smell of dead wood came over him, and something big and black crossed the sky up high. A new smell grew here, too, wild and different. It was the dampness of moss, but uglier. And, yes, there *were* shapes in the sky—things he couldn't make out, but gliding dark things that made him picture big-assed manta rays that could fly.

A weird cry came from the distance, and the girl gave a worried glance over her shoulder.

"What the hell is that?" he said.

He looked back to the shimmering surface that hung at the tree. It was like a hole in space, a gate maybe, a thing out of Narnia or the old *Portal* video game he had played the shit out of back when he first got his system. The dogs had backed down, and he could see a clear path back to #26.

"I gotta get back or I'm gonna get fired."

"What you *gotta do*," the girl said as she stepped in front of him, "is learn that when I *say* get your ass up, I *mean* get your ass up." She grabbed him under the shoulders and with a single heave, yanked him to his feet.

He was maybe an inch taller than her.

"Lannie's gonna kill me," he said, trying to play off his embarrassment.

"Will you *shut up* about going back?"

The darkness closed in on him, and the girl pulled him away.

He ran with her, still too stunned to take much in, but also both pleased and mortified by the fact that she was holding his hand. It felt like high school, the two of them running through the woods together. But that image faded quickly because this was like no high school woods he had ever seen.

It was dark and damp.

The trees were burned out and shattered. The sloppy ground shifted under his feet as he ran in his heavy clogs.

A branch ripped at his shoulder.

Vines moved at his feet.

He wanted to pull away from her, but the raw fear of pursuit from something he couldn't see made him flash on *Blair Witch Project* meets *The Cabin in the Woods*.

The stark moonlight reminded Jon of the night he was arrested, that moment when flashlights flooded the alleyway where he sat huddled in his dark corner like the defenseless little prick he had been. Fear lived in these woods. The cold promise of annihilation hovered over him like a flock of buzzards just out of sight.

A rasping sound came from the distance, a sound that made him picture hordes of insects scurrying over dry creek beds. Movement flickered at the edge of his sight.

The girl hurdled a dead tree and waited while he did the awkward lunge it took him to slide his way over it.

The process left him covered in dirt, and her beyond annoyed.

His chest burned, and his lungs ached for air.

His legs were made of noodles.

Jon had once run track in high school, but that was a long time ago now, and to call him out of shape was like saying Hannibal Lecter might be a little touched in the head.

They kept running.

Black rats the size of pigs were racing beside them now, angling like defensive backs trying to save a touchdown. Their eyes glowed fiery and red. Their teeth clacked. Their high-pitched chitter made his stomach crawl.

It was too much.

He wanted to take a breath. For just a single goddamned minute he wanted everything to just hold the hell on.

Instead, he followed the girl as she ran an obstacle course marked by tree stumps and dead brush, his footsteps still thick and lumbering. He glanced over his shoulder. The presence of a bat-shaped mass of darkness dropped toward them and drove a shiv of ice into his heart.

This was no goddamned game.

Darkness swooped from the sky, close enough now that Jon thought his chest might explode. A pain-filled screech came from above, and Jon stumbled, putting his hands to his ears.

The girl dragged him along.

Her eyes glistened in the darkness. The wiry muscles of her shoulders and arms bunched in the moonlight. Her face contorted when she pushed him forward.

"Run, you lazy piece of shit!" she screamed.

It was perhaps the only thing she could have said that would get his feet moving again.

This is fucked up, he thought as they crashed through the woods. *Totally crazy.*

As she ran, the girl turned and spoke a flow of words Jon couldn't understand. She waved a hand at the beast, and her palm pulsed with purple light. The same exotic aroma that had come from her book filled his senses, and the dark beast screamed as it made a sudden turn, twisting away like a fish in water, leaving behind a massive gust of wind and the *whomp* of a blanket being pounded by a broomstick.

The girl stumbled but kept moving.

More of the rays flew overhead.

They came to a clearing with a single tree standing at its center. She led him to its base and Jon fell with his back against the tree, panting as she drew her dagger. Creatures poured from the darkness around them, chattering with eerie screeches that clogged Jon's brain. There was no way, Jon thought. No way could one woman with one dagger stand against this horde.

A dark, human form came forward whipping a bladed weapon against the darkness.

The girl twirled the dagger in her hand, then turned to the tree and used the point to trace an outline along the trunk. Lines glowed with orange fire as she swiped the dagger up and down across the bark, back and forth.

A passage opened, and golden-sheened light streamed from below.

"Go!" the girl yelled as she shoved him down the passage so hard he fell over the earthen stairs, bruising his knees and scraping his elbow as he came to rest, then picking himself up to run farther.

His legs hurt, and his thigh burned from a bruise he knew was already rising. The abrasion from where her fingers had dug into his shoulder still stung, but mostly Jon was now Officially Scared As Hell. He ran. Just ran on pure auto-pilot, putting one foot in front of the other.

The stairs spiraled downward.

A thin network of roots glowed from the smooth walls, casting golden light strong enough to see by.

The ground rumbled as the "doorway" closed above them.

The girl followed him down, their footsteps giving thudding echoes in the enclosed passage.

They descended until the stairs opened into a small room.

He saw no other doors or passages.

Perhaps a dead end should have worried him, but the only thing Jon could do right then was to … thank … the holy ... Mother ... of God … that this run was over.

He leaned over and sucked air as if there might never be air again.

A sledgehammer pounded inside his skull. His chest burned like he was breathing acid. He collapsed into a nearby chair, thinking he might be about ready to puke up his spleen.

"Never again," he wheezed, holding his stomach. "I am never … chasing … a girl … again."

The girl, too, sprawled, panting, into a chair.

The idea she might die on the spot, however, didn't seem to be a pressing concern for her.

The room around them had a few chairs, and a low table covered in more books like the one the girl had left in the park. Golden light glowed from the recessed ceiling, but the walls were also lighted by a lattice of the same roots that had covered the stair-well. The whole thing was like a surrealistic bird cage, like a block that had been cubed straight from the center of the earth, a strange landlocked shark tank, the corners sharply cut and smelling of rust.

"Jesus," he gasped. "What are you trying to do to me?"

"It's called *'saving your life,'*" she said. "I hope you're worth it."

"Well," he said, pausing for more breath. "I think … you suck at it."

He would have said more, but he was too busy scraping oxygen to do anything beyond think indiscriminate swear words in her general direction.

The girl sat up.

"Take a minute or two and get yourself together," she said. "We've got a lot to get through and not much time to do it in."

A few wisps of her hair were plastered to her temple with sweat. Her long arms—marathoner's arms, Jon thought—rested on the chair. Her eyes flared in the golden light, and the tips of her green hair, even matted to her head, shimmered with waves of color as she moved. The body art that ran down both arms burned with a mesmerizing essence that made Jon's own shoulder itch.

Even as scattered as Jon felt, she was still the most remarkable thing he had ever seen. But he also had to admit that this amazing girl—who could leap dead tree limbs in a single bound and who could throw bursts of fire that fought off flying manta rays of death—scared the total shit out of him.

"What the hell were those things?" he said, calming down enough that his brain kick-started again.

"Those things," she replied, "are *daemons*."

"Son of a bitch," Jon replied. Though he had seen a couple billion of the things in video games or movies, he had no idea what a daemon was. "Are we in Hell?"

"No," the girl said. "This is Fae Realm."

As if that meant anything to him.

"You might have heard them called other things," she said. "The unseelie, or dark fae maybe."

"Or not," he replied.

"Doesn't matter," she replied. "They are what they are. You'll just have to get used to them."

On the wall across the room, Jon saw another spectral view of Forsyth Park, this one focused on the white fountain. Sunlight bathed the scene. People were walking through the park. Water sprayed in the breeze. Thinking it might get him the hell out of here, Jon stood and stepped to the wall to put his hand on the image. The surface resisted his hand, though, like a projection screen.

"That's not a gate," the girl said.

"Those are the same dogs," he said, putting his palm on the wall where the image of the animals retreated.

"Yes," she replied. "Though, in reality, they're daemons, also. Or at least they're being controlled by daemons—the man, too. In the right circumstances, the Dark Court can control anything that lives."

Jon gave a deranged laugh. "This is completely insane."

Rumbling came from above.

Jon's eyes grew wider. The low ceiling gave him the claustrophobic sense of sitting in a bomb shelter, which was probably truer than he wanted to know.

"Are we okay here?"

"We're on a ley-line," the girl said as she also stood up. "That's a place where magic runs strongest. So the wards should hold—at least until the Dark Court takes this zone, or as long as Antone doesn't do anything stupid for a while, which admittedly may be asking a lot."

"I hope you won't be offended if I say that doesn't make me feel any better," he said.

She took him by both shoulders, and Jon thought she was going to shake him. Instead, she just stared at him with her deep brown gaze.

This close she smelled both warm and spicy.

"I want to answer all your questions," she said. "But right now I need you to calm down."

Jon took an exaggerated breath, knowing he was beaten.

"I'm not good at taking directions," he said.

She gave a crooked smile he loved. "Neither am I."

"Already noted."

The girl opened her mouth to reply, but a voice came from the other side of the room first.

"W hat do you think you're doing, Micaela?"

A male stepped from the corner, dressed in a form-fitting jacket and a pair of dark leotards that made him look like a rebellious ballet dancer. He was like the girl, but even more so: taller, and more angular. Everything about him gleamed. His skin was satin-smooth, and his hair was a metallic wave of something that was almost silver. In short, the man looked like a pewter version of David Bowie.

He wore a rapier at his side, and as he stepped forward, a series of sigils embroidered into the shoulders of his jacket flared with blue fire.

The girl—Micaela, Jon assumed, now—stood up and took a firm pose.

"*Someone* has to deal with the bridge," she said. "And you're too busy playing hero to do it."

Pewter Bowie set his jaw, then scanned Jon up and down with an expression of such contempt that it would have made an airline security cop jealous. The corner of one lip ticked up, and a depth of examination came to his steel green eyes. His head tilted back.

"You've been obsessing for *years* over *this*?" he said to Micaela.

"Don't you have anything better to do than to check up on me?" she replied.

"You should listen to your own advice, little sister."

The male gazed at the image of the park.

"The decision has been made, Micaela. The bridge is not important—and even if it was, pulling your human plaything into this war is the wrong way to deal with it."

"He's not human," she countered.

"He has human blood."

"No more than I do."

"Oh, Micaela," the man replied with a slow smile, standing even taller than before. "I'm sure you'll understand exactly what I mean when I suggest that your lineage is not a good standard right now." He cast a peculiar glance toward Jon. "Though, given your bloodline, one can come to expect these kinds of dalliances."

The girl's eyes narrowed.

She arched her back and used meticulous care as she crossed her arms into one of the most direct "fuck off" poses Jon had ever seen.

"You are treading a very fine line, Antone. If your father was here he would have your hide."

Antone narrowed his gaze to match hers.

"You're probably right," he said, "but my father is not here, and neither—as you so well know—is *our* mother."

Jon couldn't take any more of this.

"I'm right here," he said, standing up to bring the conversation to an awkward halt.

He was shorter than the male, so he had to look up to him.

"I've come too far to be treated like dog shit," he said. "Who the hell are you two?"

He turned to Micaela. "And what do you mean *not human*?"

The three of them stood there until Pewter Bowie turned to Micaela.

"You know the council will banish you?"

"Not if I'm right, they won't."

Antone's chuckle was a weapon.

"Who would have guessed," he said, "that after all this time you would finally grow an actual spine."

Micaela said nothing, but her eyes grew tight with ire and her jaw clamped down.

"It's your life, Micaela," the man said. "Just keep him out of my way."

He looked at Jon.

"Welcome to the Green Army, mate."

Then he waved his hand and disappeared, leaving behind a scintillating haze that faded out like something from a damned Star Trek movie.

———

J on stared at the empty space, slack-jawed again.

Anger colored Micaela's face, and she raised a boney hand to her forehead. For a moment Jon thought she might break down and cry. Instead, she just shook her head.

"Welcome to the Green Army?" he said to her.

She sighed.

"As if we needed an extra load of crap today, right?"

Jon laughed at that and felt better for it.

"That," Micaela replied, "was my brother. Half-brother, actually. You're going to have to be careful around him. He's the most egotistical asshole who ever lived, but he also happens to be leading our defense."

"Defense?"

"There's a war on, if you couldn't tell," she said. "We are not winning."

Jon sat down, and sighed.

Micaela stepped over to him and planted her boots in front of his chair.

"Let's start this over. You're Jon Hale. I'm Micaela Alandari," she said, holding out her hand.

He looked at it, but didn't move.

"You know my name?"

"Don't be an asshole," she said, pushing her hand at him. "Of course, I know your name. I've been watching you for a long time. I'm truly sorry things are turning out this way—but I'm not the one who sent the daemons after you."

Her grasp was dry and warm.

It made him happy.

He liked how she smelled, too—which made him think about the crap smeared all over the front of his uniform, which then made him feel like even more of an idiot than he already was. At least the stuff was dry, and most of it flaked off when he stood to brush it away.

"So," he said in a voice that sounded no more settled than he felt. "What is this place, some kind of bastard child of *World of Warcraft* and *Final Fantasy*?"

"That would be cool, wouldn't it?" Micaela said.

She paced back to the wall where the image of Forsyth Park still played.

"Alas, we're not there. Instead, we're in a place called Crystalwood. But it's all part of Fae Realm, which you can think of as a parallel world next to the Harshlands if you would like to—the Harshlands is what the fae where I come from call the human world. But I think it's better if you think of it more like Hogwarts."

"You know Harry Potter shit?"

"Who doesn't?"

He shook his head, and Micaela continued.

"Like everything else, though, it's more complex than that when you get into the details."

"Fae Realm. At least I know not to freak out when I see Alice or Frodo," Jon deadpanned.

"Sarcasm," she replied. "I'll take it for now."

He snorted. "So, you're like, a fairy?" he said, standing again because sitting while she paced was uncomfortable.

"No," Micaela said. She put her hand to her head. "Crap, this is going to be hard."

She turned to him.

"What do you know about human faelore?"

The question caught Jon off guard. He wanted to say something more adroit, but only a few simple images came to him. "Faelore? You mean, like they dance at midnight at Stonehenge, and drink and eat, and ... well ... get a bit, uh ... randy?"

"Yes," Micaela said, smiling at his discomfort. "That's what I mean."

"I guess that's about it."

"Good."

"You think it's a good thing that I don't know what you're talking about?"

"Your ignorance means there's less to reprogram. Human lore is a hodge-podge. It's jumbled up a lot of what the fae actually do."

"So you're saying the fae *don't* dance and drink and … uh … whatever?"

"Well," she said with a grin that he felt down to his toes. "That part's kind of right. But there's a lot more you need to know before it's all said and done, and the fact that I don't have to deprogram you also means I can stick with what you need to know right now and let the rest flow as it comes along."

He chuckled.

Despite all this weird crap, he couldn't help but find everything the girl did to be attractive in ways that went beyond … well … beyond anything else he knew. Yes, she was pushy *and* aggressive, but she was pushy and aggressive in a Rebel Without a Cause kind of way that made him feel good. Now that Flying Manta Rays of Death weren't threatening to eat his shit for lunch, the part of Jon that wanted to impress this girl was beating out the part that wanted to yell at her for ruining his life.

Just be cool, he thought.

Don't be an idiot.

Unfortunately, he was so confused right now that he had no trust in his ability to not be an idiot.

"All right. So, I'm all ears. What exactly is a fae?" he said. "Not human, I take."

She laughed.

"No. Fae are not humans. Get that right, or someone's liable to take those ears of yours right off." Micaela paused. "For now let's just start by saying the fae are like humans but twice as volatile, a hundred times more passionate, and with the ability to touch magic that humans can't."

"I see," he said, not really seeing.

"As you've seen with Antone, a lot of true bloods can pass for human—at a glance, anyway. And those of us who are less than true bloods can almost always slip into the Harshlands without skipping a beat."

He nodded. He wanted to ask Micaela's full heritage but couldn't find a polite way to do so.

"But," Micaela said, "where humans on the whole would prefer to make things, the fae prefer to play politics. You can consider intrigue as the fae version of football."

"I take it you haven't seen a presidential election around here?"

"Yes, I have seen elections here," Micaela said, brown gaze boring in on him. "And they do not come close to comparing to the nastiness that spawns from Fae Realm. Someday it's going to be very important for you to understand how the fae system works. For now, though, all you need to know is that the realm is divided into a gazillion courts, but that when things get totally shitty, all the various courts roll up into one royal family."

"And let me guess, things are shitty now?"

She raised an eyebrow. "War on, right?"

"And the Dark Court is, I assume, the enemy?"

Her smile brightened. "And Antone said you were going to be stupid."

Jon grunted. "Are the Dark Court fae, too?"

"The dark fae consist of fae who have been 'turned' as well as an encyclopedia full of strange creatures who live in the magical climes of Fae Realm. Their politics are different—let's call it less sophisticated at this point, and leave it there. Their magic is different, too. It can be powerful, but it's a lot less complex, which can make it less useful for certain things."

"Magic," Jon said, remembering her work earlier.

She nodded.

"Does this mean it's possible you could wave your wand, or whatever, and take me back to my van?"

"Enough with the bad idea."

"I'm talking hypothetically."

"No, you're not."

Jon blushed hard. "You can read my mind?"

"You wish."

He didn't know what to say to that, so he sighed.

"Look," he said. "I really am sorry, but this truly is a big-assed deal for me. I mean, like, if I don't go back right now, my boss is going to take a special kind of joy in firing me, and if that happens, my life is literally done. I could seriously be on the streets."

Or worse, he thought. If Lannie canned him, it could get very bad.

Micaela's face grew hard.

"Trust me on this," she said. "Going back to your van is a very bad idea."

"I can give you the number of a certain probation officer who would be very happy to argue with you on that."

"You saw the daemons, didn't you?"

Jon sighed. This was too damned crazy.

It wasn't fair. He had finally got his act together after dealing with the fallout of his own goddamned stupidity, and after dealing with all the shit from his mom, who had made his life hell before drinking herself to death. He was figuring it out. He had a job now. He paid his rent. And on top of that, the music thing was at least halfway happening even if it would never wind up anywhere near where he wanted it to.

Sure, he lived paycheck to paycheck, but at least he had that much.

Now this.

He put his hands up.

"Okay, look. I'm done now. Just get me the hell home. I absolutely admit that I came around because I wanted to get to know you. But this is just waaaay over my head. I don't care how interesting you are: there's not a chick in the world worth this kind of crazy."

Micaela's eyes grew an edge. Then she gave something that might have been a smile under other circumstances.

"Yeah," she replied, "that's real sweet of you. And we can talk about who's a *chick* later. But as much as I appreciate a good back-handed compliment, I need you right now. And that means you need to get right with the idea that you *are* here, and that there's nothing you can do to change that."

"You need me?"

"I'm thinking you might help me save the world."

"You've got to be kidding me."

"I know how you're feeling," she said.

"Why me?"

He flinched as another rumble came from above.

The ceiling light flickered, the ground shook, and a cloud of sod fell to the floor.

The entire place seemed to close in on him then. Jon couldn't take it anymore. He looked for a place to run.

"Looks like I was wrong," Micaela said.

She dug her fingers into Jon's arm, and he shook her off without thinking.

"Calm down," she said. "Take my hand."

The room shook again. The smell of soil grew sharp. The view of the park went dark, and this time large chunks of earth crumbled inward.

Rather than take her hand, Jon raised his arms to protect his head.

"All right," Micaela said. "We'll do this the hard way."

Then she launched a body block that sent them both flying, wrapping one arm around his neck and the other around his waist as they fell. She spoke a consonant-laden stream of sound that made the bottom fall out of his world

… again.

Out of the Woods

T his time the fall was just far enough that Micaela's weight punched his breath away, and he cracked his skull a good one against the hardwood floor.

He blinked against the sunlight and found himself in familiar surroundings.

His apartment.

It was a crappy second-floor dive over a restaurant on Congress Lane, just south of Ellis Square. It looked over Rocko's—a bar where first-gig indie bands appeared on Tuesday nights. He found the apartment due to a guy in a band and, for that same reason, paid only half price. He'd lived here for a whole six months, but still hadn't gotten around to buying shades for the windows, so the afternoon sun exposed a layer of dust on the floor that got kicked up into clouds of motes when Jon and Micaela fell on it.

Despite the fact that his heart still raced like it was in the Daytona 500, it felt hellaciously good to see something normal again.

It also felt good to have Micaela sprawled on top of him. Her frame was warm and her smell delicious.

A pair of pigeons, startled by their arrival, flapped away from the open window.

He smiled up at her. "I never knew you cared, my dear," he said.

She gave him a big grimace and rolled off him. "I didn't save your ass just because I needed a boyfriend."

"I'm sorry," he said, feeling like a dork.

He sat up and rubbed the sore spot at the back of his head.

The room was hot—his air-conditioning was about as reliable as a promise from the mayor, and it cost an arm and a leg, which is why he generally just left the window open.

"I thought you said we couldn't come back here?"

"No. I said it was a very bad idea."

As she took in his apartment, embarrassment made him grimace.

"Don't look too hard," he said as he stood up. "The place is a total wreck."

"You can say that again."

He stood up and grabbed a dirty T-shirt off the back of a chair, hoping the pizza box at the edge of the derelict card table he used as his dinner nook would somehow up and disappear.

The small sink in his kitchen held the pot he'd heated spaghetti in the day before. His sofa was a dilapidated monster he found at a garage sale. A month's worth of mail spilled across his "coffee table," which was a just pair of bare planks supported by milk crates lifted from a store a few years back. He had a tablet, and a game system plugged into a small TV—with one controller tossed into a corner of the couch, and the other sitting on its side next to one of the crates. The walls were plastered with flyers from local bands.

He couldn't help but notice the odor now, which, while not over-powering, was, nonetheless, an unpleasant shade of … well, let's not go there.

"I don't usually have visitors," he said.

"I imagine not," she replied.

He grimaced.

The truth was that he *did* have girls here, but it was usually late when they arrived, and they were often not the kind that came for his digs. The people he hung out with were still on the grittier end of the bar crowd—as dangerous as that might be for someone like him. His entire life had been a series of strange situations, but every one of them paled in comparison to the mind-bogglingly insane fact that right now a girl from Fae Realm was standing in the middle of his living room.

Micaela went to the window to case the street below.

The sunlight made her eyes look like brown gemstones and her hair flash with green fire. The tone of her skin was like nothing he had ever seen. She stood in the window like a sentry, feet planted with defiance, her hands on the sill like she was claiming the place. The breeze picked at her hair.

She was so different from him.

Where he was bedraggled, she was bold. Where he was empty, she was vibrant. Where she had ideas and plans, all he had was the desire to make it to the next day.

And, yet.

There was a time, not even so long ago, when that hadn't been true.

As a boy Jon was going to be a space pirate, and that one summer in high school he and Kasey had worked out the logistics of an entire trip to roller board across the country. He and a couple schoolmates formed a band for a while. They sucked, but they had fun and he got to write crappy poetry and daydream about jet-setting around the world.

He had been bold back then.

Despite all the strange shit in his life, he had, at one time, expected things to get better.

When had he given that up? Before the drugs, or after?

As the sun cut lines of Micaela's face into his brain, Jon realized it didn't matter *when* he gave up his ability to dream, only that he had.

Jon stared at her, skewered by the stark and obvious understanding of exactly how stupid he was.

He wanted to impress her, wanted to be strong around her, but

Micaela's sense of purpose was intimidating. It made him feel like a bog full of quicksand.

And *that*, he realized as he stood in the middle of his crappy little apartment, was not *her* fault.

Micaela turned to him.

"The Dark Court can find you here," she said. "Go get changed."

Jon stood there like a stooge, unable to respond.

"Are you all right?" she said.

"Yeah, I'm fine," he replied too quickly. He looked down and saw he was still in his blocky brown uniform.

"Then get to it," Micaela said. "I'm serious. We need to leave."

"What should I wear?"

"Anything will do. It's probably best that you can move, though. So something loose. Do you have any weapons?"

"Just a pocketknife."

"I'll give you one of mine later."

"Are you going to tell me what's going on?"

"Change first. I know a safer place where they won't be able to find you. Not easily, anyway. We'll go there."

Jon frowned, hesitating as he rubbed the back of his neck.

She crossed her arms.

"Don't make me come over there," she said. "I don't care how pretty you are, if it comes down to that I can guarantee you will *not* like the result."

"All right," he said, stopping at the doorway to his bedroom. "But don't think that I missed the part where you called me pretty."

"I owed you a backhanded compliment."

"You win," he said, raising his hands.

He ducked into his room.

It was a tiny space with a few plastic bins for his clothes and a mattress that sat on the floor. The sheets were wadded against the wall, making such an uninspiring sight that Jon was just as happy that Micaela wasn't seeing it.

He changed into cargo shorts and a black T-shirt with a Green Lantern logo.

"You're into music," she said from the other room.

Jon stuck his head around the corner and saw her peering at his wall of promotional flyers. He had Kaz, the Street Moms, Clash of the Living Dead, and a whole slew of others up there.

"Yeah," he called as he carried his Nikes and a pair of socks into the living room. "It's kinda my thing."

Micaela squatted down in front of the only thing in the room he had spent any time organizing: his book stand.

"What are these?" she asked.

"Magazines and newspaper clips mostly," he said as he pulled on socks.

She looked at him with the obvious request to say more.

It made him feel good.

"All things I've written."

She pulled a copy of *Rock Club* out of the stack. It was a very small publication that had moved to the web since they had released that issue. He'd reviewed Silver Clad Jesus in that issue. They hadn't been half-bad, but Lillie Kamden, their lead singer, had gotten herself roughed up in a car accident two weeks later, and the group faded out.

The intensity Micaela studied the pages with made him uncomfortable.

"You appear to be quite the name."

He shrugged. "Ah, yes," he replied in a radio voice as he spoke into a shoe like it was a microphone. "Jonathan Hale, our intrepid critic of Savannah's underground music scene." Then he bent to put the shoe on.

It *was* true, though. To the outside world, he was a bit of a presence in the local scene.

Not that Savannah was any big-assed deal.

Relative to the real world Savannah was a very little place. It had "sludge metal" to its name—an acquired taste at best, but at least that was something. It's fans were fervent, too. Savannah couldn't make a band, but it could make a band feel good about themselves—something just about as important. And as such, that made Jonathan Hale who he was: a medium-sized fish in a small-sized pond, a guy with a certain cachet, and, in a strange way, a guy whose troubles with addiction gave him a weird form of gravitas.

He wasn't exactly Lester Bangs, but he could drop a name or two.

As he glanced up to watch her scan the article, he thought about how few of the other girls who had come here ever took the time to read anything he did, and how, even when they did, he had never really cared.

Micaela was different, though.

Her attention made him uncomfortable because he wanted her to like his work.

"Nice," she said as he pulled on his second shoe.

"Thanks."

"Is this what you want to do?"

"What?" he asked. "Write?"

"No, deliver boxes."

He laughed.

"I like music," he said. "And I like writing. So, yeah, I suppose I would do it full time if I could."

She nodded. He couldn't tell what she thought, but her interest made him happy.

"Maybe music is like my version of magic," he said, sitting upright, and feeling like a massive poser even as the words were leaving his lips.

Micaela didn't react to that, though. Instead, she looked at him in way that stripped open his soul. "Then why don't you do it?"

He grimaced and stood up.

She didn't let up, though.

"People write about music for their living, don't they?"

"Sure. Some do, anyway."

"Why not you?"

"The landlord likes it better when I pay the rent."

Micaela put the magazine back and stood up, too. "There are times," she said, "when you just have to decide what you want, and then do it."

Jon grumbled.

"I'm serious," she said. "Sometimes that's the only way to make a change. Decide what you want and go do it."

"Is that what you're doing now?" he said, remembering her conversation Antone. "Making a change?"

She smiled.

A loud thump came from the window, and a blast of fear froze his spine.

A blob of something ugly and black sprawled on the hardwood floor.

"What the hell—" Jon said.

The creature was half-dragon, half-bat—an awkward-looking thing about the size of a soccer ball that righted itself with a lurch, then pulled a webbed wing out from where it landed. It had a mouth full of razor-sharp teeth.

"The pigeons were monitors," Micaela called, reaching for her weapon.

The creature lurched once more, then launched toward Jon.

Her knife looped through the air and hit the beast with a force just strong enough to send it off course.

The dragon-bat hit the pizza box and slid off the table to crash down onto the floor.

Jon picked up a wooden chair and drove one of the legs into the creature. It gave a garbled squawk, and the chair broke with the force of the jab.

The dragon-bat tried to get away, but Jon hit it again, twisting the chair in mid-stroke to use a second leg, which also broke.

The release that came with the attack was like a glorious bolt of lightning. It felt good. So goddamned good, crashing the shards of the chair down into the blackness again and again—so good to throw all of his confusion over being powerless, and over probably losing his job, down into the creature—that he pounded on the beast over and over again, the sound of crunching wood filling his ears. The rush of blood pulsed through his body, and the shrieks of the dying creature sliced through his mind.

When he was done, an oily splotch of dead mess covered the floor, oozing black grossness that Jon assumed was blood.

He looked at Micaela, his chest heaving, hands shaking.

A dead dragon-bat was lying on his dining room floor.

The shit was real now.

The Dark Court knew where he lived.

"Crap," Jon said.

He dropped the remains of the chair, feeling messed up and so embarrassed he would have paid a week's salary to just disappear from the spot. He didn't want Micaela to see him like this.

"We need to go now," she said as she retrieved her knife.

He was no longer arguing.

They left the apartment and rumbled down the stairs, his steps once again feeling thick and cloddy compared to hers, but at least his cross-trainers made him feel more comfortable than before and made it easier to keep up with her.

The heat outside was like a wall of water, but her pace created a breeze strong enough to cool the sweat on his brow. They walked east at first, then south, toward Orleans Square before ducking into the Coffee Fox, an upscale café at the corner of Whitaker and Broughton that had an elegantly painted placard advertising coffee, pastries, lunch, and even craft beer.

He tried to center himself as he followed, but nothing registered except the dead thing that he could still picture rotting away in his apartment. Micaela said these things were hunting him—a fact that he was now absolutely forced to believe.

But why?

Why the hell would anyone be interested in a twenty-two-year-old recovering addict who drove a goddamned delivery truck?

At the Coffee Fox

A wave of air-conditioning hit as she led them into the café. The waitress told them to sit anywhere.

Micaela touched the front door as it closed, and gave what Jon might have taken as a quick prayer if he hadn't been paying her real attention. But he caught the spark that snapped when her fingertips touched the glass. It was a ward, he thought. She had just cast a protection over this place. At least it was a comfortable lie. The idea of being safe anywhere right now would be hard to accept otherwise.

The place was all glass and wood, with a tile floor.

The aroma of baked goods hit like an invisible fist, and Jon was suddenly hungry.

The sound of a latte machine gurgled behind the counter, and customers prattled in the background. The people here watched as Jon and Micaela picked their way to a table. *No*, Jon thought. The people weren't watching *them*—they were watching *her*.

Jon's invisibility to the naked eye made it easy to get into the nooks and crannies of various clubs, but he found it annoying at the same time. People didn't ignore him so much as they didn't find him significant enough to pay him any attention.

Micaela—with her hair and her body art and her physical movement that had a certain sense of beautiful awkwardness to it—was the kind who drew attention.

They took a table halfway back, oriented to give a view of the street.

He sat, fighting equal urges to be angry at her for dragging him into this thing and wanting her to take them to some uninhabited island out in Fiji where they could live the rest of their lives together.

"I assume we're safe here?"

"They'll keep looking," Micaela said. "And they know we're in the area, so I'm sure they'll canvas it. But they can't sense us directly now, so they'll have to find us on hoof. I would say we're as safe as we can be right now."

"Great," he replied. "Now I feel a lot better."

"Just keep your eye out."

The waitress came.

Jon couldn't help but canvass the street outside.

"Coffee," Micaela said with a smile. "Cinnamon and brown sugar. *Lots* and *lots* of brown sugar. And a muffin. Maybe blueberry?"

The waitress, a tall black woman with a neon smile, wrote it down. "Good choice," she said.

"Same," Jon added. "Only no sugar, and no cinnamon."

The waitress looked at Micaela and tossed her head his way. "He doesn't know what he's missing, does he?"

"Doesn't have a clue," Micaela said with a grin. "But he's all right anyway."

The two women laughed while Jon peered out the window and looked for something big and ugly that wasn't there.

This day was a complete disaster.

The waitress went back to the counter.

"I didn't come here to be made fun of," he said when it got quiet.

Micaela put her elbows on the table, and hunched herself down. Her hair fell over her eyes, and her lips became pouty. "Well," she said, "then I guess it's time for you to pull your big boy panties up and grow a pair."

He gave a soft snort.

"You don't take much shit, do you?" he said.

Micaela turned her palms up.

"What you see is what you get."

He gave an actual smile. "Well," he said. "What I see looks pretty interesting," he said, wincing at both his own dweebishness and the way it caused her demeanor to take an almost audible step backward. "For example," he said, indicating her shoulder. "That's nice ink."

"Thanks," she said.

The invisible shield dropped a bit, and she turned one arm toward him. The image was green vines and lavender flowers over a branch. "It's about my family."

He smiled. "I've got the tree of life on my shoulder."

She tilted her head in a quizzical expression.

"Really?"

"Did it after rehab. Wanted something to remind me that someone has to be at the base of everything that happens."

He didn't often expose himself like that, but the words found their way out before his brain could put on the stops.

"That makes sense," she said, nodding to herself.

"What do you mean?"

The waitress returned with their order. Ceramic plates and metal spoons clattered as she put them on the table.

"There you go, hun," she said, laying the bill on Jon's side. "You make sure to hold onto this one, hear? She's a cinnamon and brown sugar girl. That means she's special."

"Believe me," Jon said. "I know exactly how special she is."

The woman grinned, then left again.

He sipped his coffee and grimaced when it burned his tongue.

"It helps if you blow on it."

"Uh-huh."

Micaela prepared her drink with maybe twenty buckets of sugar, held the cup in both hands, and took a sip.

"Umm," she said, closing her eyes and letting the concoction do its work. "That's yummy."

"I'm glad," he replied.

He looked out the window and saw pigeons on the roof ledge of the building across the street. He put his hand around his mug and shuddered as he thought of the dragon-bat in his apartment.

"So, isn't it about time you told me what the hell's going on?"

"Yeah, it is. You're not going to like it, though."

"You mean like I've been so *loving* everything else today?"

"Touché." She gave a crooked grin and drank more coffee. "I'm serious, though," she said. "This is going to get weird."

Jon stared into her gaze with a combative flare.

"You're going to tell me I'm fae, aren't you?"

He would have liked the approval that came to her expression if he wasn't so unsettled.

"Your father was from Fae Realm," she said.

"My father left before I was born."

"How cliché," Micaela said.

Her piercings gleamed in the artificial light as she bit her lower lip and stared at him.

Jon pushed his chair back and watched people stroll along the sidewalk like this was just a regular, everyday moment. He had known it was true the moment she had first said it to Antone, but things had moved so fast.

A pickup rolled down the road playing Kenny Chesney. Sparrows bounced around the concrete looking for any stray chips that diners who sat outside may have left behind. A surge of paranoia hit like a baseball bat to the gut. A kid on the corner caught his eye and, at first, Jon imagined him as a daemon. Then the light turned and the kid crossed the street.

"I've never been normal, have I?" he muttered.

It was a question, and not a question.

"Did my mother know?" he said, once again in a low tone.

Of course she had known. She had to have known.

Didn't she?

His response was weighted toward anger steeped in something

self-righteous as hell but was a sensation too new to name. The past year had been a desperate attempt to just be *normal*. Now he didn't even know what normal was.

He poured more coffee and looked at the menu, trying to be okay but pulling a complete and total epic fail.

A full minute later, he looked up.

Micaela had eaten her muffin while giving him space to think.

"All right," he said, pressing his palms to the tabletop. "I'm sure there's more."

She leaned in.

"Everything starts a couple hundred years ago. Early 1800s. Here in Savannah."

Jon nodded.

"There was a man, a white man, who had a child with one of his women slaves. It was a boy, and when that boy grew up he was, as they said back then, quite fetching—so fetching that my mother took a liking to him."

"Your mother?"

"The Fae live a very long time." Her smile widened. "I was born just before your Civil War."

Jon sipped his coffee and enjoyed the burn as it crawled down his throat. He didn't know how he felt about this news.

"You don't look it," he said.

"My, my," she said, fanning herself with one hand. "If you aren't the silver-tongued devil."

He shrunk back. She was confusing.

Everything was confusing, but that was just life—first you're born, then you find out your father's a deadbeat fae, then you stick your foot in your mouth with the hot immortal girl who saved you from daemon dragon-bats. With any luck he would wait awhile to get to the *then you die* part, but right now he wouldn't bet the rent on anything.

Micaela grinned, then reached over and broke off a piece of his muffin before continuing.

"Since the fae do actually like the dancing and the drinking and the, uh, merrymaking," she paused while a mischievous light came over her face, "my mother stole this young man away to Fae Realm. This was a problem, though, because my mother was already committed."

Jon smirked. "Women."

He shoved the half of his muffin that remained into his mouth and washed it down. The food made him feel better, and if he was honest with himself somehow the idea that he was half-fae was settling in and beginning to make a lot of the crap he had been living through come together. Now he just had to figure out what it all meant.

"Her love was real, though," she said. "If it *wasn't*, I wouldn't be here."

He stopped with his cup in midair.

"You're saying this guy was your father?"

"That's exactly what I'm saying. You and me. We're both half-fae, which happens, but usually just because of simple flings, which are fine, but not fine. The fae have strange relationships with celibacy, monogamy, and sex altogether, very open, but also very … well …"

"Political," Jon said.

"Yes." Micaela's entire body lit up in a way that pulled at every molecule in Jon's body. "Political, in every way possible. If my father had just been a fling, no one would have said anything, but when my mother made it clear she intended it to be a long-term thing, the rest of the family revolted and forced my father back to the Harshlands."

"Racism: alive and well in Fae Realm?" Jon said.

"Technically speciesism in this case," she replied. "The fae didn't care about the color of his skin, only that it came wrapped around a human being."

"I see. Still sucks."

"Anyway, short-sighted self-preservation isn't some kind of superpower that belongs to humans. All the 'isms' exist in Fae Realm, too, some even stronger than here."

"I understand," Jon said.

"Then you're one of the few."

He picked up a packet of sugar, put it into his coffee and stirred, not sure what to say.

"Since their love was true, I suppose she followed him here," he replied.

"She wanted to, but she had two problems—the most obvious being that she's the queen."

"Excuse me?" Jon said. He stared at her as a truth slowly formed in his mind. He leaned in to speak in a lower tone. "Your *mother* is the queen of Fae Realm?"

Her nod was so slight he almost missed it.

"So you're a princess?"

"You'd think that would be a big deal, wouldn't you?"

"Sounds like a big goddamned deal to me."

"And it would be. Except, you see, I'm the *queen's* bastard daughter, not the *king's* bastard daughter—which makes a whole lot of difference. It's not a thing when the *king* makes an illegitimate kid, but when it's the queen there's no end to the distress."

Jon turned his palms upward. "Life continues in its suckitude."

"Yes, it does." She ran her fingers over the edge of her cup. "Anyway," she said, "her other problem was that as much as true fae do enjoy their time in the Harshlands, human mortality wears them down. They belong in the realm. Sometimes they try to live here, but they always come back. My mother couldn't stay, though she wanted to."

"Humans do better in Fae Realm?"

"No guarantees, but generally, yeah," Micaela said. "Human lore is right in that it's not unusual for fae folk to steal human lovers and keep them stashed away forever."

"Hmm. Sounds like a tough life."

"There are worse things that can happen to a person. But it's good to remember that there can be a very fine line between a privilege and a prison."

Jon thought about that.

"Then, of course, there are half-bloods—like us—who get along in both realms but don't really belong to either."

His lips gave an involuntary twist.

He had said those words—*I don't belong here*—a hundred times to the hundred shrinks and social workers who had been assigned to his case. They had never understood him.

"So I'm fae and you're a princess."

"Check, and check."

She sipped coffee, then began again.

"When I was born, my mother returned to the Harshlands so my father could see me. That's when she learned that—because of his time in the realm—he had been listed as a runaway, and that his master had beaten him so badly he had to be taken to the hospital, which was no boon for a slave and black man back then. While he was waiting for treatment, he caught the yellow fever and died.

"She found his remains heaped into a pile with the bodies of other slaves and dropped into a hole, then covered over."

"Jesus," Jon said.

"His graveyard is marked by the fountain."

"The one at the park?"

She nodded. "The bodies were buried right before they built it."

"Son of a bitch," Jon said, feeling a sense of *déjà vu*. "I must have sat against that thing a hundred times."

"It gets better."

Jon waited.

"My mother took me home, then returned to bond with my father's remains by casting herself into the fountain's water."

She gave a half-smile that urged him to catch up.

"You mean … your mother is *in* the fountain?"

"It was the only way to keep his essence alive."

"I mean, like … she's still there today?"

"Yes. My father, too—she's in the fountain, he's in the park—the trees and grass. They live together in the twee-space between realms."

"That's freaked out," Jon said.

"Maybe so, but the magic that bonded them is based on true love: the strongest power there is. It's nearly unbreakable."

Jon nodded, letting it settle.

"All right," he said. "I admit this is all interesting, *and* weird …

and I really don't mean to be an asshole here, but … I still don't see what this has to do with me."

"I'm getting there."

He rolled his eyes, and as he glanced out the window the daylight darkened as if the sun had gone behind a cloud.

Into the Water

A chill of recognition prickled Jon's spine as he recognized Trice Smythe standing at the same corner where the kid had been.

Smythe was a big guy, round and jovial in his baggy shorts and his tent-like blue button-down, a guy who could talk a mile a minute and always had a smile on his face despite looking at you with a pair of eyes that shifted back and forth like they were connected to a damned metronome.

Smythe was one of his old dealers, a guy everyone called "BR31" because he could get you about any flavor of anything you wanted and because he used it as a handle on every form of social media in existence.

Right then Trice Smythe was talking on his phone. His eyes flickered toward the café.

"Goddamnit."

Jon pulled back to hide behind the window frame.

That's when he saw Micaela frowning.

"What is it?"

The doors at the back of the restaurant opened, and two people entered—a pair of rocker girls dressed in stained jeans and tank tops, hair dyed in shocks of purple and red, cut in a windswept fashion that left it to fall down one shoulder. One was tattooed on her wrist. Both clomped across the tile floor in high-heeled boots.

He'd seen the type before, girls who hung around the clubs.

He recognized something else, too.

They were fae.

He sussed their essence now the minute he saw them.

"Put money on the table," Micaela said. Her eyes grew wide, and her lips set into a line. "Now."

She stood up as the girls came to their table.

The blonde of the pair—blonde with purple streaks—blocked Micaela's path, while the dark-haired, scarlet-streaked creature stood in Jon's way.

Up close they smelled of body odor, and the thin veins in their eyes were visible. Their dilated pupils combined with their swagger to give them a dangerous edge.

The girl before Jon wore jeans that were ripped at the hip.

Dark fae, he thought, knowing it was true in some way he couldn't explain. These were fae who had been turned by the Dark Court. His skin crawled with the thought.

Jon dropped cash on the table and also stood.

Outside the window, Trice Smythe appeared to be staking out the front door, phone still held to his ear.

"You're not going to do this here, are you?" Micaela said to the blonde fae.

"That's completely up to you," she replied. "If you come with us the restaurant doesn't have to go up in flames." Her gaze flickered over Jon before returning to Micaela. "He's not really that useful anymore, is he?"

The blonde fae was in control, Jon thought. She was the leader, the brunette the sidekick.

Jon's nemesis put one hand on his shoulder and ran the fingers of her other down his chest. Her lips pulled back in an overtly carnal expression.

"I can find something to do with him."

Jon flinched, but a part of him couldn't help but respond to the heat of her body as she pressed up against his side and the light sensation of her hand on his breastbone.

"Keep your hands off him," Micaela said.

"What is this?" the blonde said. "Jealousy from the half-breed princess?"

The other laid her temple on Jon's shoulder. "Well," she said as her hand slid to his belly. "He is very pretty."

"Anything more I can do for you two?"

All heads turned to see the waitress returning with a fresh pot of coffee in one hand and a porcelain bowl of cinnamon in the other.

She had seen the commotion, Jon realized, and came to check the table in hopes of defusing things before they got out of hand.

Jon took advantage of the moment to palm a fork from the table.

"We are fine," the blonde said. "You can go—"

Micaela slapped the bowl of cinnamon, sending it flying into the leader's fae's face, who gave a surprised yelp as she clutched at her eyes, and spun away, falling halfway into a chair.

The waitress, surprised, tripped and spilled hot coffee. The pot cracked as it dropped to the floor.

Micaela spoke a word of magic, and the chair slid away, screeching and stuttering under the fae's weight.

The fingertips of the fae beside Jon dug into his arm, but he pressed the fork hard into her ribs.

"Another move and you're dead," he said.

She froze.

"Come on," Micaela said to Jon.

Jon stepped around the woman, keeping pressure on the fork and feeling the movement of the woman's breathing.

She closed her eyes and gave a deep smile.

"I can teach you many marvelous ways to use that," she said with rawness in her voice that drove a shiver up his spine.

Micaela pulled Jon away and gave the fae woman a glare that would scald a normal person.

"Anyone in this café gets hurt," she pointed a finger, "and I will hold the two of you personally responsible."

"Don't be foolish, Micaela. Even you know that this daemon is already out of the bag."

The back door burst open again.

A musclebound man in a tight T-shirt and dark glasses stepped into the room. Jon recognized him at first glance—the guy who had held the dogs back. The man held up his hand, said one word, and unleashed a blast of power that ripped through the room with a wavering front that was like some kind of CGI thing straight out of *Inception*.

It sucked the air out of the room in a single beat.

An instant later, the explosion was deafening.

Tables scattered. The shock wave picked up chairs, trays, and cups, and created a whirlwind of napkins, uneaten food, and utensils. The force hurtled Jon through the room. Every pane of glass in the place shattered. Jon flew through the air. Time seemed to stop. Detritus hung in place—a woman's bag, a paper place mat that doubled as a coloring page, broken chair legs—then everything let loose and the power of the blast threw him onto the rough concrete of the sidewalk outside.

He landed hard with a pile of glass and wood and broken porcelain.

Micaela lay beside him, dazed and bleeding from a cut on her temple.

Son of a bitch!

He got up, half crawling to her side. She was bleary-eyed.

People were reacting now, voices trilling in the way they get when something terrible has happened, but no one knows why.

Jon grabbed Micaela under one armpit and dragged her to her feet. She wobbled and staggered but somehow kept her feet under her.

Behind them, Mr. Muscle picked his way through the wrecked restaurant like some kind of Schwarzenegger clone.

"Hey, man!"

Jon turned to see Trice Smythe stepping across the street, shoving his phone into the billowing folds of his shorts.

He took two steps forward, and punched Trice in the nose,

dropping him like a 250-pound bag of meat. Then Jon grabbed the back of a chair to Frisbee it at Mr. Muscle, watching as the chunk of wood caught the brute at the corner of his temple, and he too dropped like a brace of steel timber.

Jon was surprised it worked but didn't wait to see if he got up.

He put his arm around Micaela's waist and pushed her down Broughton Street.

"Come on," he yelled.

They ran down the sidewalk as fast as he could push her, picking their way past tourists, and crossing in front of a van, ignoring a horn that blared into the afternoon heat.

As they ran, Micaela began to curse, then cursed more and more, until after a few paces she was spewing a streak of blue language that seemed to get her back into being the same Micaela that Jon had so recently grown to know and … uh … love.

A block later, he let go of her, and she was running on her own.

She wiped a trickle of blood from her eyes, and spoke a few words. The smell of her magic rose.

"That should slow them down," she said.

Another stream of blood trickled down her face.

Jon's legs ached from before. His thigh felt like a block of concrete, and his right arm burned from his landing on the sidewalk. They slipped into the cover of a hedge-lined block that surrounded a museum of some type. A wrought iron fence painted black lined a park ahead of them. They rumbled past green-painted benches and over hard grass.

A siren rose from the distance behind them.

First responders, he guessed.

No one seemed to be following as they left the park, but Micaela didn't let up.

She ran down a path that led them to a complex of low-rent apartments painted white and gray and with roof tiles that had been sun-beaten from red to orange.

"Can we … slow the hell down?" Jon said.

"No time," Micaela replied, pointing ahead. "North!"

"I can't do it," he said.

She glared and he kept going.

This was a quieter section of the city, shaded by rough-growing trees and with grass that grew in equal crops of crabgrass and rye. The streets had the afternoon silence of a place where working people live—the construction folks, the people who clean houses and fix broken pieces of the city as it wears down. It was off the beaten track, a place no tourist ever went—a place hidden in plain sight.

Their feet echoed in the emptiness of the street.

Jon's forehead ran with sweat, and his heart pounded in his chest.

More sirens howled in the distance. Engines roared.

He didn't have much left to give, though. His entire body hurt, and his knees wobbled as they made a sharp turn.

They crossed Bay Street, passed the post office, and went north.

In the distance, Jon heard a barge horn and saw the arching white crest of the Talmadge Bridge, complete with its complement of cars that inched over it as if they were little automaton ants.

They came to a chain-link fence with rusted razor wire looped along its top.

The Savannah River rolled past on the other side.

Squealing wheels came from behind.

A bright yellow muscle car of some type fishtailed, rear wheels smoking, engine warbling as if the devil himself was giving it a hundred lashes.

Mr. Muscle from the café twisted the wheel, and the car careened toward them from two blocks away. The dark-haired rocker chick sat in the passenger seat, her long hair fanning out in purple streaks as the car slid back and forth.

Micaela ripped the bottom of the fence up, pealing it up like a banana and leaving a gaping space to roll under.

"What are you doing?"

"Go," she yelled.

Jon ducked and rolled into the gap.

The car engine screamed, and Jon thought he heard Micaela's voice calling magic again.

She bent the fence up harder, then rolled under it herself.

She was up and running again before Jon got off his knees. She grabbed him by his sore shoulder and dragged him with her.

The river bed was fifteen feet away as the car blasted through the fence.

Jon slipped on the mud.

Micaela shoved him headfirst toward the water.

"Dive!" she yelled.

He screamed and put his hands out like he was falling into second base as he went airborne. A freeze-frame image of the river flowing beneath him locked itself into his mind.

The smell of cinnamon merged with the reek of algae.

Then someone hit fast-forward, and the water's chill slapped against his body as he skipped on the water.

Once.

Then twice.

The third time, the river engulfed him.

A symphony of bubbles and foam rushed over his ears. Pressure built around him like a band of water wrapped around his chest. He smelled fish. Saw dark shapes hanging in green space, their jaws gape-mouthing, their eyes black and staring with stoic observation.

He could breathe, though.

Even under the water, the bubbling water parted enough that he could breathe.

He sucked air and kicked his feet as the current took him into darker water. The motion was like being on a tram, very automated, projecting him forward without effort.

The water sounded like it was boiling.

But he could breathe and he was moving in a direction away from the car that was loaded with Mr. Muscle and the fae.

With nothing left to do, Jon kept his hands pointed over his head and rode it out.

Onto the River Bank

When the rushing of water subsided, Jon found himself waterlogged and bent over on all fours on the opposite shore. His hands and knees sunk into the fine, mushy-soft silt that lined the river bank. The sounds of the flowing river formed around him one source at a time—the dripping of water, the call of a bird and the buzzing of a dragonfly in the reeds, rustling of sawgrass from the shoreline. Cars hissed in the distance as they drove across the Talmadge Bridge, which now rose in a majestic white arc above him. He tasted mud and something that was almost brine.

As he rolled over to sit up, a guttural scream rang across the riverscape.

"I'm going to kill the asshole!"

Micaela sat in a couple of inches of water maybe ten feet away, panting for breath, but still cursing a streak.

She was as soaked as Jon was, her green hair pasted in a smooth cascade that shimmered with iridescence in the sunshine.

"He's gone too damned far now!"

She pounded the river. Muddy water went flying.

Her face flushed and drew into a sharp expression Jon hoped to never be on the wrong side of. She got to her feet and kicked up another shower of river water, then balled her fists, bent over, and grabbed a big chunk of driftwood that she then used both hands to fling out where the current ran fastest.

"You hear that, Antone!" She kicked at the water. "You can't fucking do that!"

She glanced around and saw Jon.

Her jaw set, and she took a breath.

"Are you all right?" she said, raising a hand to shield her squinting eyes from the sun as it moved toward the horizon. The tone of its color made her skin blaze.

Jon was afraid to answer.

He did his best to ignore the fact that her wet clothes revealed more of certain parts of her body than she might be comfortable with. His best, however, was less effective than he was proud of.

From the other side of the river, the yellow hood of the car was visible in the water. The dark fae and the muscled man stood on the shore, both with their arms crossed, the man's sunglasses dangling from one hand.

Jon looked at Micaela, then their attackers.

"Are they coming?"

"Not right now," she said, gritting her teeth. "Right, Naheemi?"

The surface of the river nearby swirled.

A figure rose from the turmoil, the upper half of a torso made of pure water, bald and fae-thin, glistening in the sun. It gave a quiet bow toward Micaela, then disappeared back into the river.

"What the hell was that?" Jon said, meaning the creature.

Micaela, however, kicked the water again, smirked at the sight of the sunken automobile, and then waved to their pursuers before returning to take in Jon.

"That," she said, "was fucking politics."

Realizing he wasn't going to get anywhere until Micaela finished doing whatever Micaela was going to do, Jon crawled out of the river and collapsed onto the trunk of a downed swamp palm. His water-logged shirt clung to his chest and shoulders. His pants dripped with sludgy river water.

His entire body throbbed like it had gone through some kind of hot press. The news that Mr. Muscle and the rocker chick weren't going to be Star-Trekking their way over here to pound on them in the near future served to help him breathe a bit easier, though. And, to be honest, the fact that he had actually punched his way out of the café made him feel better about himself.

Like maybe Micaela would think he could take care of himself —or at least be able to pull his own weight.

He was half-fae, after all.

Maybe he should start acting like it.

Of course, that idea just made him feel stupid because how the hell does one begin to act like a fae?

He pulled off a shoe, hoping he could get the grey-black silt out of it. The river inside smelled organic.

"A hundred and twenty dollars down the goddamned tube," he said.

He felt around his pockets. His phone was toast, but at least he still had his wallet.

Without warning, he flashed on the idea of #26 still idling in front of the Oglethorpe Club, and laughed out loud. The idea of being upset at being fired seemed quaint in a way that would have been unimaginable just a few hours ago.

Helluva day, he thought.

Micaela lingered at the water's edge, kicking an empty plastic milk bottle that had washed up there. The river had cleaned her wound, and she was no longer bleeding, but anger still colored her face.

She joined him on the stump, though, still shaking.

Her hair clung to her shoulders. Wet and in the shade of the clearing, it was the color of evergreen trees. Beads of water rolled down the curve of her neck. Her clothes clung to her trim body as firmly as his clung to him.

He ignored the coarser responses his body made to her closeness by focusing on his second shoe.

"Good move with the fork," she finally said.

"Thanks."

She pulled off one of her boots and used more energy than necessary to toss it up onto dry ground. The other boot joined the first, then she sat there without speaking, wriggling her toes as the world came to its proper speed again.

"What was all that about?" Jon said.

"It was about my asshole brother and how I'm going to fucking kill him."

"I don't get it."

She put her left hand out. "This is Antone," she said. Then she did the same with her right hand. "This is dead."

She glared at Jon.

"What's not to get?"

He waited.

"How do you know it was Antone?"

Her shoulders raised and fell with a deep breath.

"Those two fae girls work for him."

"The two rocker chicks in the café?" Jon drew his eyebrows closer. "I thought they were dark fae."

"The guy was, but the girls were with Antone."

"I don't get it. Your brother is head of the Green Army, or whatever, isn't he? Why would he be working with dark fae?"

"Of course you don't get it," she said with a sharp point. "You *fucking wouldn't get it* because—" she gritted her teeth "—it makes no fucking sense that he would fucking do that."

She stood up and paced.

"Only, of course, this is Antone we're talking about."

"Clearly you need a little more time to calm down," Jon said.

"Don't tell me what I need."

Jon nodded, raised his hands in surrender, then pried himself off the stump to take off his shirt and wring it out. He had more productive things to do than deal with a distraught fae girl. As he twisted the fabric, river water splattered in the silence between them. That finished, he shook the shirt out and laid it over the far end of the stump so the wind could get at it.

His pants were wet, too, but that wasn't happening.

He sat down again and saw that police vehicles had arrived at the car across the way. Mr. Muscle and the fae were long gone.

"I'm sorry," she said. "I need to handle these things better."

"It's all right."

She followed his lead and wrung out the tail of one side of her top, then the other.

"Nice ink," she said, returning his compliment from earlier as she sat next to him again. She pointed to his bare shoulder.

"Thanks."

He waited a moment, letting the fresh air cool his skin.

"Are you ready to talk about this?"

She nodded. A few strands of her hair had dried and were blowing in the breeze. The various shades of green in her hair combined with the browns in her eyes and lips to give her skin the tone of honey. He smiled at that. One of the things he liked most about looking at Micaela was that her skin tone changed so much with her surroundings.

"Maybe you can start with what the thing in the water was," he said. "And then move to why Antone would want to kill us."

She sighed.

An expression crossed her face that made Jon realize she wasn't looking forward to this.

"The water fae is a gentleman named Naheemi.

"He's very independent as fae go, but he's always been a friend of mine. Knows the river better than anything else alive.

"I suppose his work was what let me breathe underwater."

Micaela nodded.

"He lets me stay here often, and he watches over me when I do—he makes sure I'm taking care of myself. In a lot of ways he's the mother I never had—though if you ever tell him that he'll toss a fit. He can control the river, though. No fae will cross it if he doesn't want them to.

"He's also the one who will get us back across when we're ready."

"And the deal with Antone?"

She glowered at the mention of his name, but corralled herself.

Micaela puckered her lips and moved her head back and forth as she contemplated the question.

"You're a challenge to him now," she said.

Jon shook his head and ran his hand through his wet hair. "No offense," he said. "But how does an out-of-work delivery guy compete with the guy who's leading the Green Army's defense of Fae Realm?"

"Well," she said, her hesitation palpable. "That's the problem, right?"

She put her hands to her sides, then straightened her arms so her shoulders hunched around her neck. She rocked back and forth like a skier prepping for a downhill run, then let go a sigh.

"I've been trying to think about the right way to say this for years, really. But there just isn't a good way to do it."

While Jon waited, an uncomfortable feeling niggled at the pit of his stomach. It was like sitting in a doctor's office or waiting in a quiet little courtroom for his public defender to come in to explain The Plan. He didn't want to hear what she was going to say, but he was incapable of turning away.

Micaela spoke.

"Antone wants you dead because your father is the King of Fae Realm."

He sat there, feeling the rubbery essence of the what-in-the-hell-are-you-talking-about expression that covered his face.

"It's true," Micaela said. "I've been watching you since you were born."

Still, Jon remained silent.

"No one in Fae Realm pays much attention to a half-blood, so I've always been able to dig into things that others don't seem to care about. I followed my step-father on one of his trips here, and saw him tryst with your mother."

Jon laughed then. It was a high-pitched giggle more than anything else.

"Tryst with," he chuckled. "There's a hell of a euphemism."

"I was trying to lead up to it more kindly," Micaela said, "but it is what it is."

"What it is, is ridiculous."

"It's the truth."

"I don't …" Jon paused, shaking his head. "I still don't … I mean … even if it's true, why would Antone care?"

"You're number two in line for the throne, Jon, so you're a threat just by drawing breath. He wants you out of the way."

He blinked, still trying to comprehend what this meant. The smell of the shrubs and weeds that made up the nearby wetlands seemed intense now. A bee buzzed nearby.

"But I don't want to be king of anything," Jon said.

"That doesn't matter."

"You serve even if you don't want to?"

"You can step down, but intrigue runs deep in Fae Realm. No one will believe your decision is real."

"Great," he deadpanned.

"I told you. Fae politics are a blood sport. I protected your existence for so long because the news would make you a target, and, to be honest, because if I told anyone, my stepfather would kill me. But you look very much like him, and I'm certain that once my brother put eyes on you he knew the whole story. Now that The Little Asshole knows you exist, he wants you dead."

Jon recalled the edge to Antone's glare while they had been in Fae Realm.

"That much I can believe."

"I'm sorry."

Jon stood up and took a few barefoot steps forward, feeling the wind blow against his chest and taking in the skyline of the city.

Son of the Fae King.

It was impossible, right?

But … Jesus.

It felt good just to think it.

Strange.

And scary.

But good.

One of his counselors had lectured him once about how he had "won the genetic lottery" as a white male, and how the world was stacked in his favor. Maybe that was true, or maybe not, but at the time Jon had just about screamed at the guy. Jon didn't give a shit about society. Jon cared about Jon, and as far as he could tell his genetics hadn't done a damned thing for him. Now the idea that he was the son of a fae king made him boggle.

Was he like, Superman or something?

Micaela came to his side.

He pushed his drying hair out of his eyes.

"Can I do magic?" he said.

"I can teach you some, but how much you learn depends on a lot of things."

"I don't know what to do with this."

"I understand. But I'm warning you—even after you get a grip on who you are, you've barely cracked the cover, and that's even before I get around to kicking Antone's ass."

He looked at her.

"All right," he said. "Tell me what I need to know. If this is going to happen, let's do the hell out of it."

Her smile was magnificent, part pride, but also parts of things that could be interest, challenge, or even just pure wonder. He realized then that he meant something to her, but he couldn't decide what that something might be. He saw things inside her that he hadn't seen before. Micaela had grown up as a half-blood in Fae Realm. A girl without a mother. A girl with a step-father who didn't pay attention and a brother who was now willing to kill her. And he saw more, too, confusing things that he couldn't interpret.

She still scared him, but now he thought that maybe he could handle it.

He wanted to get to know her more than ever.

"All right," Micaela said as she put her hands on her hips and stood taller. "We have a lot to cover before it gets dark."

He laughed.

"What?"

"You look like an elven Wonder Woman," he said. "All you need is a tiara."

She shrugged and crossed her arms. "I'll take that."

He nodded. She could probably rock the tiara thing, too, but he decided not to tell her that.

"Why before dark?" he said.

Her smile was a combination of wry and clever. "You'll see soon enough."

"Is that code for 'Here comes Miss Bossypants'?"

"If you like it that way."

"I like it whatever way you like it," he said.

She glared.

"All right." His 'lips locked' symbol made her smile.

Micaela began.

"Everything I've told you so far: the fact that you're part fae, the crap about faedom, and the story of my parents—even, to some extent this new thing about The Little Asshole Antone (which will now and forever be his name until I kill his ass)—has been basic stuff, simple background you need to understand the rest."

"Great."

"So let's go back to the war in Fae Realm for a minute."

"An oldie, but a goodie."

She glared again, and again he did the 'lips locked' thing.

"Some are saying it's going to be the bloodiest war we've ever had. But it's a war our council says will end with us winning."

"But you think they're wrong."

"I think the council is stuck in the past. The core of Fae Realm's power comes from a wellspring deep inside Golden: our cornerstone city, and a fortress so strong the council believes nothing can possibly take it. So they've decided to fight a war of attrition by waiting there until the Dark Court destroys itself against its walls."

"From your earlier comment, I assume it's worked in the past?"

"That's right. It has."

"So…?"

She sighed. "Failure breeds change, Jon, and the Dark Court has always lost."

He liked that she seemed to be releasing her thoughts as an actual sharing, as if she were trying to explain her thinking rather than trying to educate him. It made him feel closer to her.

"So you think they're going to do something different."

"Exactly."

She put a hand on his arm to accentuate the answer.

"I wasn't really certain until now," she continued. "But given all the crap happening around you, I'm convinced that the Dark Court is working to add firepower by bringing in new resources. If I'm right, both the fae and human cultures could be on the verge of being destroyed."

"They're using the bridge," Jon said.

Micaela rewarded him with another expression he immediately fell in love with. "How do you know about the bridge?" she said.

He shrugged, feeling like he'd been caught out. "I don't know what you mean by it, but you mentioned it while you were arguing with, uh, The Little Asshole Antone."

She set her lips into an amused line.

"Ah. You were listening."

"Yes," he said. "I was."

He didn't know whether the 'listening' she referred to was his use of Antone's new nickname or the fact that Jon remembered the conversation about the bridge. Regardless, a few other words from that first conversation flashed back to him. Words like: *plaything*, and *obsessing over*. But his brain was already struggling to follow everything else. Those words would have to wait.

Micaela continued.

"Small groups of fae usually cross between the worlds at places where lines of power intersect," she said. "But there is a place where, with the right kind of magic, masses of people can now pass at the same time."

"A Bridge to Fae Realm," Jon said as a black bird glided over the shoreline and landed in a mangrove tree near the mouth of a nearby tributary.

"Yes," Micaela replied.

"Are you sure we're all right?" Jon said, staring with caution at the bird.

"It's just a bird this time."

"How do you know?"

She shrugged.

"Once you get some time to settle into who you are, you'll be able to tell better yourself. I'm glad you're thinking like that, though. It's possible they could try to fly something across the water, but I'm guessing that now that surprise is gone, they'll hold their resources for the end-game."

"I suppose that makes sense."

To be truthful, nothing made sense, but in a world where nothing made sense, he guessed that made as much as anything.

Jon sat back and collected up the conversation.

If Micaela was right about the Dark Court attempting to find new "resources," and if they planned to use the bridge, that meant they either intended to send a mass of daemons here or take a mass of humanity into Fae Realm.

Or both.

"You're saying the Dark Court plans to use humans to fight the war?"

"At last!" Micaela gave a toothy grin. "Someone who can see the big picture."

He frowned. "But, no one's going agree to do that."

"The Dark Court will turn them—or at least enough of them. Those who fall prey won't even know what's happening."

Jon thought about Mr. Muscle and the dogs.

"This is like some weird Tarantino take on *The Grinch Who Stole Christmas.*"

Micaela turned to him.

"Here's the kicker," she said. "The woods at Forsyth Park *is* the bridge."

"Of course it is," Jon said.

"The power of the bond that connects my parents is what created the passage to begin with, but it also served to lock it so that no one can cross—either way—without a key, or without breaking the bond."

"I see where this is going," Jon said. "The Dark Court is stymied as long as the nexus is locked."

"Bingo."

"So they're trying to break it?"

She nodded. The breeze had dried them off some, and she had to brush a few green strands of hair from her face.

"That's how I come into this, isn't it? You need me to stop them."

"Well … yes and no."

Jon grimaced.

"What the hell ever happened to *what you see is what you get?*"

"The Dark Court wants to break the lock," she said, ignoring him. "But to do it, they have to remove my father's remains."

"Dig up his bones?"

She nodded.

"Well now," he said. "Doesn't that sound like something that would be a complete blast to do on a Saturday night?"

"The problem they have in doing that, though," Micaela said, using her voice to scold him, "is that only a person of the blood can break a bond made of true love."

"You mean a descendent?"

"Right—a direct descendent of the queen, like The Little Asshole Antone or me," she said with a firm gaze, "or someone less direct, like anyone else with fae blood who might also be connected to my father."

The combination of her pause and her stare told him what she meant.

"I'm not—"

Micaela's expression bored into him.

Jon put his hand to his forehead as he took a couple steps away. He didn't know how much more of this he could take.

"My mother?" he said.

"Seven generations back," Micaela replied. "Her line leads to the man who owned my grandmother."

"And he …," Jon looked to her. His stomach dropped about ten floors in an instant. His face drained.

"He was my biological grandfather."

She paused.

"That makes no goddamned sense," Jon said. "Your stepfather?

Having a fling with the ancestor of … ? It's too much of a coincidence."

"Oh, it was no coincidence." She gave a biting smile. "It's a very fae thing to do—tryst up with relatives of the lovers of a past mate."

"That's sick."

"It makes a statement. He's still angry with my mother. He's been made a fool of, and has never forgiven the fact that she's with my biological father."

"So it was revenge?"

"Exactly."

Jon drew his lips tight.

"More relevant to the topic at hand, though," Micaela said. "It all adds up to mean that your heritage gives you the ability to move my father's bones, just like mine does."

"That's why these things are hunting me?"

"That's why the Dark Court *needed* you before. They're *hunting* you now because they weren't able to break you."

"Break me?"

Micaela closed the gap between them.

"I know you've had some difficult times," she said.

She put her hand on his shoulder and took him in. Her face turned to the wind as she looked at him, and the open breeze caused her eyes to narrow.

"But you need to understand that the drugs were part of the Dark Court's plan from the beginning. The magic that bonds my parents can't be broken under coercion, so they needed your consent. They pushed them your way hoping you would break. You were young. They wanted to wear down." She paused. "Once they controlled you, they would give you commands: small ideas at first, but then bigger ones until, eventually, you would find yourself digging in Forsyth Park."

Jon took a deep breath, trying to keep his emotions in check.

Could Micaela be right? Could the drugs have come from something beyond him?

If so, what did it mean?

He had taken them on his own, after all. No one had put a gun to his head and said, *'here, boy, take a ride on the X-ta-Z mega-train, or you're a dead man,'* right?

Yes, that was all true. He had to own it.

What he did was his fault.

But the idea that the Dark Court had pushed it made everything feel different.

"Trice Smythe …" he said, recalling how powerful he had felt when he punched his dealer in the nose.

He clasped his hands over the top of his head, closed his eyes, and turned his face away from the sun.

Infinite darkness filled the space behind his lids.

He remembered voices, the maniacal whisperings that came as he drank beer and whiskey in clubs, or as he snorted lines of powder. He flashed on the edge of being high, the night he stole a guy's phone, and another when he bet a girl fifty bucks she couldn't walk the ledge on a downtown building's roof. He remembered loud music that tunneled into his brain to calm him down. That music had saved him, he thought. It had brought him back—though it was almost too late that last time.

Micaela stepped closer and put her hands on his shoulders.

He couldn't meet her gaze.

Falling into his addiction was the most embarrassing thing he could ever imagine. It had stripped him of every shred of his self-respect. It had taken him to his knees, and made him weak. The drugs had ripped away every one of his dreams.

"You beat them, Jon," Micaela said.

In the darkness of his own thoughts, the individual touches of each of her fingers were separate things across the top of his shoulders. They held him there like anchors.

"When you chose the facility, you showed you were stronger than the Dark Court."

He remembered the moment he decided to put a stop to it.

He had not been strong that night. Instead, he had been cold and shaking so hard he thought his muscles were going to rip themselves apart. Cold in that concrete cell, square, with its peeling paint and its shit-stained toilet open to the air. He had been alone, and in more pain than he thought he could ever stand.

He had lost everything.

Now this amazing woman was telling him that he had actually been strong. That he had actually won.

It was now officially too much to handle.

The whole fucking day. Too much. To fucking. Handle.

The heat from her touch warmed him. He smelled cinnamon and brown sugar over the fresh scent of open air.

He looked at her, blinking away dampness that had collected at the corner of his eyes. Her chest rose in a slow breath. Her eyes were wide and dark, her lips firm-set and fine. The artwork on her arm pulsed and he felt better, but then he wondered if he just made that up.

She broke contact as he wiped his eyes, but she remained close to him, close enough he could still see the amber-brown glow that the redder rays of the fading sun burned into the finer hairs along the slope of her neckline, and close enough that the slight difference in their height caused her to tilt her head up to meet his gaze— which she did now, connecting her eyes to his to ensure he didn't slip away as he moved on. The twitch of her smile gave him strength.

"This is too damned freaky," he said.

"It's the truth. It's also the main reason I couldn't tell anyone what's been going on. My step-father would have exiled me to keep anyone from finding out he had accidentally created a bloodline that could damage Fae Realm. It could be bad for a lot of people."

"You could have at least told *me*."

"Fat chance," she said. "First, you wouldn't have believed me. But beyond that, I didn't know how you would react. I couldn't have you going off half-cocked and exposing yourself."

"I wouldn't have done that," he argued.

She gave a huge snort. "You romantics are the worst. Half the time you don't even know yourself what you're actually doing."

"I am *not* romantic."

She gave a wistful sigh. "Sadly, that's probably true. But I didn't say you were romantic. I said you were *a* romantic. You have passion. You live for the moment. You feel the power in things that others don't see. Your thing with music shows it."

He shrugged. "I admit there was a time when I loved the idea of living for the moment."

"See? I couldn't take the chance."

He laughed at himself. The world had closed in on him. He looked at Micaela. She looked so sincere—so there. He didn't know why he did it, but he reached out and touched her face, then pulled back with a move that made him feel awkward.

"All right," he said, bracing himself and hoping she hadn't noticed. "So the Dark Court is trying to fuck with us. What do we do to get in their way?"

She nodded, and her smile grew wide enough to expose teeth. Her gaze flickered away from him, then returned, her brown eyes glittering in the dying rays of the sun.

"Yeah," she said. "That's the guy I thought you were."

He looked at her crosswise. He wanted the tone of her voice to mean more than he suspected it did, but everything was so raw right now. He was confused, and he wasn't going to be an asshole. The last thing Micaela needed right now was a jacked-up Jonathan Hale, and then he thought about this whole thing with his family tree and hers and … Jesus, what the hell was he into?

He stepped back.

He didn't know what any of this could mean.

"I'm serious," he said. "I want to end this."

"The good news is that they aren't trying to turn you anymore," Micaela said. "The bad news is that now they just want you out of the conversation."

He looked at her. "How are they going to remove the lock without me?"

Micaela raised an eyebrow.

"They've got somebody else?"

She nodded. "Just recently."

"Who?"

"Your sister."

"I don't have a sister."

"Yes," Micaela said, "you do."

"No," Jon replied. "I don't—"

Then he pulled up. She was right. Technically he had once had a sibling.

"My sister was stillborn."

Micaela stared at him, then shook her head.

"My God," he said.

His mother had told him about her years ago, had actually used his sister as a punishment to express her deepest disappointment every time Jon screwed something up. *If only it was your sister who had lived,* his mother would say in her vodka-stained voice, *I wouldn't be going through all this shit with you.* Then later she would apologize, of course. *It was the booze talking,* she would say the next morning as she made him his favorite pancakes and poured a little hair of the dog.

A memory of his mother came to him then, bitter and bent over the stove, smoking and drinking, and living with a series of men before she got sick.

"Her name is Jen," Micaela said. "She grew up in Charleston. Your mother gave birth at a private clinic. No one knew about her because the midwife told your mother she died."

"Why would they do that?"

"There's a market for everything, Jon."

He shook his head.

"It makes sense," he said.

Micaela's expression asked the question *"How so?"*

"There's always been this hole in my life around her. I thought I was being silly, but I felt like she was with me. Sometimes I would even talk to her."

He had a sister. A live sister. A twin no less.

Holy fucking crap.

He drew a sharp breath, understanding something else, too.

"They have her, don't they?"

"She wasn't as strong as you."

He looked to where the eastern sky had grown dark. The wind kicked up, and his skin prickled. He hoped his shirt was dry.

"She's coming to break the spell tonight," Micaela said. "That's why they turned up the heat. The Little Asshole may want us dead for his own reasons, but the Dark Court wants to kill us because we're the only people alive who understand what they're doing and who believe it's a big enough problem to try to stop them."

"Isn't what Antone's doing treason or something?"

"Not if he wins the war."

"That's crazy."

"No. It's just high-risk politics. He doesn't believe the bridge will make any difference. If he wins the war, he'll keep his place."

"And if he kills his sister?"

"I've been throwing spanners into his plans for a long time. He'll be happy to be rid of me, and the people around him will understand the situation. So, yeah, in its own convoluted way, The Little Asshole's play makes sense. If he wins, he wins big."

"And if he loses?"

"If he loses, I will fucking kill him."

"You're not serious, are you?"

Her response was a smirk.

"Is that your play here? Is he why you're doing this—you want to beat Antone?"

She looked out over the river.

"I don't like to see broken things," she said. "And the fae are broken. My step-father, The Little Asshole, all the rest: they don't see that their egos are tied up in outdated ideas."

"You're a fixer," he said, laughing.

"A fixer?"

"You care about making things right, don't you. You see a problem and want to fix it."

She didn't reply.

"I bet you've made that argument about a million times before, right?"

This time she smiled in that self-conscious way people got when he uncovered something they hadn't seen about themselves before.

"What a pair we are," he said. "I'm a romantic and you're off tilting at windmills."

"Tilting at windmills?"

"Let's just say I understand how frustrating fighting the system can be."

Her shoulders relaxed.

He put his hand onto her elbow.

"I'm guessing that the two worlds need each other more than they know," he said.

Micaela nodded. "The fae side makes us magical, the human side makes us powerful. Lose the balance and everything tilts."

"I like that," Jon said. "It's like the bridge itself."

"It's something true fae don't see."

"I wouldn't suggest having high expectations for humans on that mark, either."

Micaela sighed. "Maybe that's just how it is everywhere."

Jon nodded.

"It's getting to the end of the day," he said. "I suppose we should get going?"

"Yes," Micaela replied.

He picked his shirt off the log. It was still damp.

She walked up the shoreline to pick up her boots, then sat on the stump to put them on.

"Your sister will come late in the night when the daemons can move more freely. There will be a lot of them—true daemon fae this time, ugly things like the one in your apartment, rather than like Mr. Olympia, your little girlfriend, and her sidekick."

Jon smiled with the barb. "Jealousy will get you everywhere."

Micaela rolled her eyes.

"I'm serious," she said, standing up and testing her boots with a movement that was graceful despite being all knee. "It won't be pretty."

"You're telling me we're going to have to fight?"

"Afraid?"

"Wouldn't you be?"

She smiled.

"Maybe we can spend the next couple hours teaching you some magic," she said. "And getting coffee. Lots of coffee."

"I assume we're going back to Forsyth Park?"

She nodded, pulling her hair back into a green ponytail as she looked down at him from her position on the river bank.

"There's a place where the bones are easiest to get at. We'll need to go there."

"Where is it?"

"Let it settle. I'm betting you'll know."

He ran his hand over the place on his shoulder where the tree of life was marked into his skin, looked out at Savannah's early evening skyline, and discovered that Micaela was right.

As usual.

Into the Tunnel

The Tunnel was an eerie place well before Mitch and Silvie Madison turned it into an underground nightclub.

The original passage ran from the old Candler Hospital, under Drayton Street, through tree roots, and into the center of the woods that later became Forsyth Park. It was built because waves of yellow fever took people in such masses that city leaders feared creating a panic, so they commissioned the tunnel as a place to store bodies until, under cover of darkness, they could be removed, taken to the docks, and eventually buried at sea.

The Madisons had made it wider and put in the stage and the bar, but left one of the Tunnel's original walls untouched, retaining the crumbled remains of pre-Civil War era plaster and brick. Ancient slats of the original iron spanned the ceiling, rusted and bent, but holding on. Crusty old braces were embedded there, as rusted as the ceiling slats, but still able to be levered wide if they were ever needed to hold another pallet or stretcher.

An ancient arc of burnt bricks remained visible in the old section, too.

It had long ago been mortared over, but at one time that section had been a crematory where folks unlucky enough to catch a dose, but unable to be carted away, were burned instead.

That crumbling wall was a draw.

The kids who came here were always up for whatever form of trouble they could get themselves into, of course. They wanted music, the louder the better. And they wanted drinks—lots of drinks.

But mostly they came to the Tunnel because of its stories, and what those stories meant to them.

These were the downtrodden, the dark and untethered, the kids who carried the weight of the world, the kids who smelled of incense and sweat and the smoke of whatever crutch they may be leaning on that night. The past trauma that lined these walls scrubbed them clean. The ghosts of the past gave them life in a way nothing else could. For them, the Tunnel was bravado itself, a southern counterculture "fuck you" to the bankers and the brokers who ran the outside world, and even to other kids who were not like them, other kids who went to other bars and other nightclubs that made up the "regular" circuit.

Jon had been there maybe a hundred times before.

He liked it.

The Tunnel had always felt like home.

Now he knew why.

* * *

It was pitch dark when Jon arrived.

The true darkness would come soon, though.

It would arrive with dragon-bats, and possessed daemon dogs, and birds and any one of the hundred other forms the Dark Court could inhabit. Fewer than in Fae Realm, certainly, but Micaela said they would come in numbers, and by now he knew better than to doubt her.

Still, Jon felt the sharp sense of being alive as he stepped into the club.

The raw wail of Pashi Tull's electric guitar clawed its way over a pounding drum, and Rem Nastie's vocals were almost on key. But the discomfort Jon felt as he descended the narrow stairwell that led to the club was stronger than the assault Kaz—the sludge band playing tonight—was throwing down.

He was on a caffeine rush so strong he could feel his hair, and his hands were shaking from the mounds of sugar Micaela had made him cram into his system while they were waiting for the night to come.

It was strange to know something horrific was going to happen before it all went down. His mind focused on everything at once.

If not for the ironic scattering of Confederate culture across the room, the Tunnel might have been a Euro-goth club—half pub and half dungeon. The hoppy smell of stale PBR fought against the butterscotch mist of vaping residue that coated the place. The original wall radiated its dark history, and the other walls were scrawled with bleary "artwork" made with spray paint, lipstick, and other things better left undiscovered.

Its floor was sticky.

The actual bar was your basic hardwood barrier between patrons and bartenders. The stage was down at the far end—just a wooden platform, raised up about half a foot.

It was mid-evening, start of the second set.

The place was three-quarters full.

He picked his way to the darkest corner of the bar, a place where he knew the sound cut like a razor to the throat. Kenny-the-beer-man nodded and reached for tomato juice as Jon took the stool.

If nothing else, having a glass in front of him would give his hands something to do while he waited.

As Kenny poured the juice, Pashi Tull laid down a guitar solo that could pull teeth.

Jon scanned the crowd.

He had argued with Micaela earlier. He wanted to clear the place out to keep people from getting hurt, but Micaela said it wouldn't help. Worse, she said having other people around would add chaos and make their defense easier.

"You're suggesting we sacrifice innocent people?" he said.

"I know how that sounds," she replied as she sipped her coffee'd sugar, "but, trust me on this. You've never seen the dark fae at their fullest, and it'll be just us two. If we don't win, every one of those people will die anyway. So this is the right play."

"I still don't like it."

"Can you live with what will happen if we fail?"

Her question bounced around Jon's mind as Kenny brought the juice.

He could call Micaela callous, but he admired her ability to make this kind of call. He suspected her approach was the right one, but he didn't think he had the gonads to make that decision.

He took a drink of the juice.

It tasted good.

Without thinking about it, his brain stitched together sentences he would have used to describe the moment he entered the club. The normalcy of that act made him smile.

An editor once told him that what he wrote should be "something more than a piece of crap you pull outta your ass." The goal, he said, was to write something that sounded like you ripped it straight out of the club itself. That idea was part of him now, and despite what was going to happen tonight, music was still what he was. Stepping into this chamber felt like stepping into a temple.

Jon put the glass back on the bar, and twirled it between his fingertips.

The weight of the dagger Micaela had given him lay against his thigh.

He hoped it would do something for him, because he had crapped out while trying to learn the small magics she had struggled so valiantly to teach him while they were waiting.

He was half-blood, she said, but fae was fae. He could do it if he found the right trigger.

"It comes from someplace inside," she told him. "It's hard, but once you get there, magic itself is simple enough. You just tie into a ley-line, decide what you're going to do, then do it."

He knew an understatement when he heard one, but he figured the core of her lesson was true enough.

"I've never been that great at making decisions," Jon replied.

"You will be."

There in the bar, he laughed out loud as he remembered that moment, not that anyone could hear him. Kaz was playing their anthem now, "Can't No One Else Be Me." Nastie screamed the words at a couple million decibels.

He had to figure out who he was again. Everything about today had set him back, and as he waited here for the main event to start, Jon tried to get a handle on where he was going. Assuming they made it through the night, he had a fresh road in front of him, and this time he had Micaela around. He thought he did, anyway. He hoped. The temptation to be optimistic was like a walking dream. He wanted to believe in it, but he didn't think he could afford the downside.

Jon stared at the wall behind the band.

It was such a small barrier, but that wall was what the dark fae would be coming for tonight. They would dig at it, rip at it, and tear it apart to give his sister a path to the boneyard on its other side.

He imagined the people who had built it.

Who were they? What they were thinking as they worked. Did they know what lay just a few feet further on? As they dug the path, had they known about mass graves where hundreds of slaves had been buried? If they did, what did it mean?

The questions bothered him.

Those bones pulled at him now—probably always had. But now that he knew the truth he couldn't miss the draw, and now that he knew where that feeling came from, he couldn't pretend to ignore it.

It could be funny as hell if he thought about it from the right angle, he supposed.

In a single afternoon Jon had gone from being anchorless and adrift to discovering that his father was a fae king, that his great-great-great-to-the-whateverth grandfather was a slaver who had raped his "property"—an act that created a whole line of relatives who had been busy living their strange little lives in their equally strange little multiverse for hundreds of years—*and* that he had a twin sister who was now on her way here to fucking kill him.

Talk about your instant family tree.

Just add weirdness and stir.

News that he had a slaver in his background bothered him. Maybe he shouldn't have been surprised, he was a white man whose family grew up in the south after all. Chances had been good. But the idea did surprise him, and it made him more uncomfortable than he could express.

It had been a helluva lot easier to just not know.

A guitar blast shook the walls. The drumbeat crashed.

He drank more tomato juice and thought about the people in the city above.

What would they be doing right now if they knew Armageddon was approaching and there wasn't a damned thing they could do except stay the hell out of the way of a half-human fae girl and her twenty-two-year-old rehabbing addict?

They would freak out is what they would do.

Just like he would have freaked out the day before.

He pictured Forsyth Park with its safe little paths and its rolling lunch vendors who were all just happy as hell to serve you a hot dog with a smile. He thought about the gardens and the grass and the open spaces where parents took their kids to play.

But above all he thought about the fountain and the boneyard beneath it, the mass of green-leaved trees on this side of the nexus and the blackness of the deadwood forest on the other side.

The world is big, he thought.

Godawful big.

This is when Micaela entered the club.

He had been so wrong about her before.

Micaela Alandari was mesmerizing as she stepped past the table of the three leather-clad guys who were drinking and bouncing their heads to the savage beat. She was gorgeous, completely beautiful in the way no other girl had ever been beautiful before. She moved like a dancer on stilts, and, despite the fact that she wore just her out-of-place leggings and her simple sleeveless top, every person in the room watched as she settled into a stool on the other side of the bar.

Your life can change a lot in a few hours.

There were a lot of things he couldn't pretend anymore.

He had no idea what to think about her, and he had no idea what *she* thought about *him*. The fact that he hadn't taken the time to talk to her about it made him feel like an idiot. It was so much like who he had become, and today he couldn't even blame the drugs. All he knew for sure was that the love Micaela's parents had for each other was all that stood between the human species and a worldwide premier of *Night of the Living Dead*.

As he sat in the darkest corner of this weird little bar, he wondered: could he ever love like that?

Could Micaela?

Were they even supposed to?

Jon wanted to find out, but as he thought about her he rubbed his shoulder and his mind clouded with ideas about family trees and kissing cousins and who-the-hell-else-knew-what he and Micaela might be.

Crissy Juno, a server who had worked there for a year and a half, fought her way through the crowd, her empty tray raised above her head and her body twisting this way and that to get around on the floor. Jon thought about the fact that she had a kid back home, and that she cleaned houses during the day to make ends meet.

"Hey, Jon," she said as she bent across the bar to give Kenny her orders.

She smelled of perspiration and something flowery.

He leaned over to tell her that she should find a way to go home tonight, but...

<hr>

The sharp chill came before the words formed.

Jon's skin shivered, and the hair on his forearms rose. He shoved Crissy into the far corner, knowing it was too late even before the first dragon-bat streaked out of the stairwell.

Micaela's blade spun so fast that most people didn't see it. The creature fell to the floor and slid under an empty table.

Oblivious, Kaz played on.

Another dragon-bat appeared.

Jon's blade caught it as it came off the stairs, and it flopped to the floor. A girl screamed, but her voice disappeared into the band's mayhem.

A swelling mass of creatures came through the stairwell—five, ten, maybe twenty gargoyles and imps and other things that smelled like tar and gathered into a tumbleweed of blackness that swirled in midair. More beasts scuttled down the stairs on claws, paws, and grotesque feet that left glistening trails on the floor. Woodland creatures came, too, chittering and chattering. Behind them came a pair of dark fae, their movements smooth and dancelike as they hacked their way down the stairs.

Their wail became a monotonic dirge underneath Kaz's sound.

Jon threw a barstool into the mass, then drove his dagger into the flank of a snarling beast. It raked at him but missed. A wild rodent scuttled toward the wall. A mass hurled itself into Jon's ribs and a grotesque creature flopped onto the beer-stained floor like a stunned fish.

Guttural screams rose.

People ran to the stairwells, elbowing and shoving their way out, but also serving to clog the passages.

A beer mug flew through the air.

Glass crashed all around, and a big-assed guy in black stood up, windmilling his arm to dislodge a snake-like thing digging its fangs into him. His chair fell. The table broke, and more glasses went flying.

Micaela's magic strobed like lavender lightning, and waves of burnt cinnamon rolled through the chamber.

The two dark fae fell dead, one crashing against an amplifier.

The cohesion of the attack flagged.

He hacked at an imp.

The band kept playing, their sound a deafening screech.

Something furry bit him in the leg. He ripped it away and stomped on a daemon that had been slithering toward the wall.

A black ghoul raced at him.

Without thinking, Jon raised his hand and thought about magic.

Concentrate, Micaela had told him while they sat in the café. *Don't try too hard. Just throw energy.*

He concentrated.

The steel-edged roar of Tull's guitar ripped into his chest. The rhythm of his chords mixed into Jon's thoughts. He danced with the sound, swam in its rip tides, bathed in its flames.

His stomach gave a lurch, and it felt like he was airborne.

Everything slowed down.

Decide and do! Micaela had said. *Decide and do!*

Energy built as the ghoul leapt.

He grabbed the flow, and threw it as best he could.

It missed.

Instead, the energy hit a chair behind the creature and cracked it into three pieces. The ghoul landed on a table, clacked its jaws, then leapt past him to scrabble toward the wall. Jon hacked at it with the dagger but missed with that too.

An unopened bottle of beer beaned it right in the head, though, exploding into a wave of foam.

Crissy Juno was behind the bar, throwing everything she could.

Micaela's magic flashed again.

She was defending the stage—front and left of the wall as they had planned. Mounds of gore surrounded her as she danced in some kind of beautiful martial art, blades flaring.

Per plan, Jon backed toward the stage to cover her.

Something slimy and froglike jumped into his face. He ripped it off, feeling skin tear along his cheek.

Rem Nastie stopped singing then. He swung the microphone at a daemon, and ran.

The bass player ducked as a flying dragon-bat bore down on him, and fell off the stage to the tune of an earsplitting warble of feedback that brought the dark forces to a momentary halt.

The drummer still pounded the skins, though, and Pashi Tull, who lived perpetually behind a pair of mirrored sunglasses, still wailed away on a solo that shook the walls. Without understanding what was happening, Tull pretended to shoot one of the dark fae with his guitar neck.

As Jon got to the stage, something grabbed onto his leg and a dragon-bat flew at him, maw gaping. He ripped the dagger across his leg, and crashed a pitcher of beer into the flying beast.

He saw Crissy spraying a spigot of soda water that she wielded like pepper spray. The flow didn't seem to hurt the creatures, so much as surprise the hell out of them.

The drummer caught something with his foot pedal, but he kept playing, eyes closed and sticks twirling.

Tull, however, dropped out of his solo to stand there, dumbstruck behind Jon, his scarred-up guitar slung low on his hips and his spindly little arms hanging out of his ripped-out sleeveless T-shirt like he was some kind of skeleton.

"Fuggin' A," Tull said between tympanic rolls.

This wave had passed, and the onslaught let up for just a moment.

Micaela stood there, panting with exertion and bleeding from several wounds. Sweat poured from her face. Her shoulders were slumped, and her back bowed. Coils of her hair lay in ropy green clumps that were plastered against her neck and flowed down her back.

She struggled to hold her dagger before her.

Jon wasn't faring much better.

He wiped a bloody hand against his T-shirt and looked out over the bar.

The place was a total mess.

Tables were strewn everywhere, and bar stools broken. The floor was covered with beer and shattered glass. Only a few people remained, wrestling with dark fae that were in the process of once again growing dense at the far end of the chamber.

The drummer stopped playing. He just sat there, though, as stoned as Tull, twirling a stick every few beats like he was just waiting for the next song to queue up.

Jon picked up a thick piece of chair remnant to use opposite his dagger.

The next wave came on.

Jon gave a warrior's scream as he stomped the first deranged creature to come close. He drove the chair shard into another dragon-bat. A rabid bulldog bit his thigh, and a big-assed pigeon flashed at him, taking a hunk of flesh from his arm. Knowing it was too late for anything else, he instinctively reached into himself to flash raw magic at it. This time the bird was too close to miss, and it disappeared into a cloud of feathers.

This magic was hollow, though, different from a minute ago—more like his failed trials in the café. There was no lurching and no flying. If the bird hadn't been right there, it wouldn't have done jack.

"There!" Micaela yelled, pointing to a swooping sheet of blackness that was headed toward him.

She could barely lift her hand.

She can't do this alone, he thought. *Be a goddamned fae and use some goddamned magic!*

He tried, but it sputtered again, so he threw the remains of the chair into the churning mass instead, and swung the dagger.

Something bit him.

The crush of this wave of dark fae built into a crescendo.

It was bigger than the first, made up of more daemon creatures, and more controllers.

They were going to lose, Jon thought.

It was only a matter of time.

A huge dragon-bat came out of nowhere to crash into his chest with such force that he fell with a thud at Pashi Tull's feet.

Tull stared from behind his shades, his lips parted and his cheeks slack.

"Fuggin' A, mahn," he said.

The wave of blackness raced past to splatter into the wall.

Once there, each creature opened their maws, claws, and anything else they had to dig with, and they gouged chunks of brick and mortar from the wall—scraping and screeching as they worked themselves raw.

They were ignoring everything except the wall now, sacrificing themselves like ants to rip concrete and wood away.

Jon understood then.

The beasts themselves couldn't move the bones, but they were digging the pathway.

Preparing it for …

T he daemon masses parted as the girl came down the stairs. Everything grew silent.

She was thin, like Jon, and dressed in something dark. Her hair was as white-blonde as Jon's but shorter, with loose strands cascading over her forehead. Her skin was smooth as glass and unmarked except for the tattooed image of a serpent that emerged from the neckline of her vest to slither into the hollow of her neck. Her fingers were long. Wrapped around the pommel of her rapier, a weapon that gleamed with blue and red as she made her way across the room.

Her head moved up and down and side-to-side as she faced Jon, a motion that made him think she was listening to some kind of private music that played to its own hip-hoppy beat.

Her eyes were fae, Jon thought. Like Micaela's, and like his own, but where Micaela's were deep and brown, this woman's glimmered with fire as light and as green as his were. The starkness of her appearance made him wonder how he could have missed it in himself.

She came to a stop a few paces before them.

"Hello, brother," she said.

"Hello, Jen," he replied.

Then she pulled a knife from opposite the rapier, twirled it between her fingers, and sent it whirling.

Jon froze.

The blade spun straight toward his head.

At the last moment, a feeble stream of Micaela's magic bent it away, and the weapon gave an ugly *thwock* as the point drove itself into the wall.

Everything erupted.

Jon recovered to find the daemons attacking again.

Jen and Micaela were locked in battle, their weapons sparking with fury, tendrils of magic smoking in the air that was now thick with the smell of blood and muck.

Micaela summoned strength from somewhere deep inside and unleashed a furious growl as she parried a blow.

She wasn't going to last long.

A black mass of foul beasts headed toward Jon.

He understood the play, then.

The Dark Court was keeping him occupied while his sister destroyed Micaela, who was now too fatigued to defend herself. It made sense: Micaela had power enough to stop this, Jon did not.

He screamed in desperation.

He couldn't bear to see Micaela struck down before his eyes—by his sister, no less.

A mutant insect flashed mandibles at him. He kicked its carapace in.

A lizard tried to scamper to the wall, but Jon spiked it with his blade.

As he rose from one knee, a grasshoppery gargoyle caught him off-balance and knocked him back onto the stage again, falling on him and nearly decapitating him with a snap of its chitinous jaws.

Jon drove his dagger into it and pushed it away.

Tull stared at him with that same vacant expression Jon had seen so many times before. The guitar player's glasses reflected a reverse image of the battle. Tull was a mindless void when he wasn't wailing on the beaten-up axe he still had slung over his shoulder. In a lot of ways, Pashi Tull was just like the magic Jon kept trying to cast— hollow and vapid.

"Fuggin' A, mahn," the guitarist said.

That was it.

Music.

Like almost everything else in his life, Jon's magic had come alive with the music, or at least music helped him make his magic. Whichever. Now was *not* the time to be thinking too damned hard.

Decide and do! he thought. *Decide and do!*

More daemonspawn splattered onto the wall behind them, and the sound of ripping plaster filled the area.

"Play something!" he yelled at Tull.

Tull nodded. "Yeah," he said.

But he didn't do anything, so Jon grabbed the guitarist by the kneecap and shook him. "'Break It Down'!" he screamed the name of a pile-driving song on Kaz's playlist. "Play the hell out of 'Break It Down'!"

"Fuggin' A, mahn," Tull said as grabbed the fretboard and ripped into a ragged A-chord that sent an orgasmic shiver down Jon's spine. "Let's break it the hell down!" Tull pounded out a machine gun riff, then dropped into a schizophrenic bit that was equal parts melody and solo.

The sound roared.

The drummer joined a moment later, and everything snapped into place for Jon. The room became a thing, an entity unto itself, a single book that he could read in a single glance, a story that flashed over his mind in a solitary instant.

There was:

A cold lattice made of every daemon and dark fae in the room.

A matrix of pain that came from each of the wounded.

Brilliance that blazed from Micaela with the aura of cinnamon and sugar.

The heat of raw courage from behind the bar where Crissy Juno was still hurling bottles of vodka and schnapps.

There was the wall, shuddering under the dark fae's attack. The wall that he now understood had to survive, regardless of what happened to him, and regardless of what happened to Micaela.

And there was the band: Tull and the drummer combined into a well, a wormhole that spewed raw power from another dimension. They were virtuosos, Jon saw, two men-child prodigies who spent their existence creating their own thing in their own way, making music they cared about even if the only place they could make it was down here in these dungeons.

The music they made now was a gale force wind that burned against Jon's mind like it was powered by a thousand stars gone supernova.

The band's power lifted him.

Jon screamed in joy that faded as he came back down into the Harshlands to find …

The wall bled soil and black ichor.

Dark creatures were perched all along it, holding onto crumbling cracks, ripping at plaster and eating at centuries-old brick.

Micaela screamed as a spell dropped her to the floor.

Jon's sister reached for the strength that would drive her rapier into Micaela's heart.

Jon grabbed Rem Nastie's discarded microphone.

He sang into it, screaming a flow of words, throwing down lyrics in a wild, loopy cadence that cared nothing for perfection. With his other hand, he grabbed his sister by the collar and tossed her away from Micaela.

Fire came into his vocal cords. Percussion scrubbed his bones, and the harmonics of Tull's first eight bars folded into an arcing blast of feedback. A heartbeat pulsed from the other side of the wall, and the scour of a hundred razor blades scrubbed Jon's skin from the inside. He twisted words to connect with the heartbeat and set his hands into shapes to throw power against the wall.

Daemons and dark fae cried out in unison.

Masses of blackness splattered to the floor like wet rags.

The three of them played on.

Tull roared into a second lead.

"Yes!" Jon screamed, falling to his knees and raising his fist to press the flow of power hard against the wall.

More daemonspawn fell.

Jon's vision wavered into a prismatic … nothingness … and it was as if time itself had frozen.

H e was in a forest, a simple clearing. Across the field an immense horde of daemons and dark fae lay in wait.

Before that horde was a pile of bones, and before that pile was a female fae.

Micaela's mother.

Her magic rose like a curtain of green between her and the horde. A copper breeze wafted across the open field.

Jon sensed the fountain above them and the open park of sycamore around them. The roots around the chamber pulsed with the bond between the queen and her lover.

Micaela was right.

The love between these two was both true and bold.

"This is twee-space?" he asked.

The queen smiled.

"I see you have your father's love of music in you," the fae woman said in a sardonic tone.

"What do you mean?"

"Don't be a stupid boy. You think I can't sense my own husband?"

He looked behind himself and saw Micaela lying on the floor of the club. "Save her," he said.

The queen squinted into the distance.

"My girl," she said.

"Save her," he gasped again.

"I can't," the queen said. "But maybe together you can save us all."

The portal flickered, then caught for one last moment. The queen spoke something that sounded poetic, but Jon couldn't decipher anything beyond the word "love."

Tull destroyed a riff.

The drumbeat throbbed like it was a thing itself.

The boneyard heartbeat gave a hymnal tone.

And, as Jon slid back toward the Harshlands, he understood. *Decide and Do.*

He pushed sound out of his body, a tonal phrase made up on the spot, poetry without words, meaning without form.

His voice touched both Micaela and his sister at the same time.

His shoulder exploded.

He tried to stand but his legs folded under him.

His final thought was that he had bruised his knee.

The music had stopped. Silence reigned.

The dark fae were gone.

Jon picked himself up from the stage, cradling his right arm, and holding the dagger in his left. Every muscle in his body ached.

The Tunnel was a burnt-out disaster that smelled of blood and fire, but the wall was now rebuilt, formed with the original brick and plaster that had been there before the attack.

The bridge was sealed, he thought, this time perhaps forever.

Micaela, lying on the floor, forced herself to her side just as Jen limped out of the dark corner, bloodied and streaked with grime, holding her rapier point down as she came into view. The hollow of her throat, once marked with the icon of a serpent, was now blistered and raw—just as his shoulder was, and just as he knew Micaela's arm would be.

She was heading toward Micaela.

Dark lines of power flowed around her with a chill that made Jon shiver.

He stepped between them and raised his dagger as she came to a halt.

"This is over," he said. "You can't win."

"Stay out of my way," Jen replied.

"Take another step and I'll kill you."

"Do it," Micaela called out, pushing herself to one knee. She held a dagger in one hand, but the other was now empty. "Do it while you can."

He should, he realized. Filled with the power of Kaz's music, he was strong enough.

But this was his sister.

As Jon stood his ground, sirens warbled in the distance.

She put her hand to her burnt neck. "You took my art."

"Leave while you can."

Micaela let out a warbled squawk. "No!"

Jen's lips tweaked up in a smile. Then she laughed.

"The Dark Court will not go away, brother. You should do what your girlfriend says and kill me while you can."

He shrugged. "I believe in you."

"No," she replied. Her expression was almost a smile. "You are just too weak to do the job."

"I used to think that, too," he said. "But I know better now."

Micaela stood and stepped forward, but had to hold herself up against a ragged amp stand to keep from falling again. Her hair slid over her face, and her shoulders sagged. The dagger dropped to the floor.

Jon stood firm.

Jen shook her head, then slid her rapier into her belt.

"I guess there's no accounting for taste," she said. She turned and hobbled through the debris until she arrived at the stairwell, where she stood, one hand on the wall and her face downcast, contemplating something before finally looking back over her shoulder at him.

Then she left.

"You should have killed her," Micaela said.

Her arm was red and raw where her body art had been scorched away.

"Are you all right?" Jon said.

"I can't believe you just let her go."

"Me either." Crissy Juno stepped from behind the bar, brushing dirt from her shirt. "I would have kicked her ass."

Jon laughed.

Upstairs, sirens grew louder.

"Fuggin' A, mahn," Pashi Tull said from somewhere distant. The guitarist stared at the wall.

It was just as it had been before, except that now, at its middle, down low by the floor, was the outline of the tree of life wrapped with a sleeve of lavender and green vines. A black serpent coiled itself around a limb at a crook of that tree, its head raised and ready to strike.

At the Fountain

J on leaned against the edge of the fountain.

Micaela paced hard enough in front of him that Jon thought she might wear a path in the concrete around it.

"I cannot believe you didn't kill her when you had the chance," she said. "Do you know what kind of damage she can do now?"

It was three in the morning and the sky was still dark except for the half-moon that hung at the skyline. Crews were working below, but the blue and red lights of emergency services had left an hour ago. The water was smooth and stagnant behind them. The aroma of sycamore trees filled the night. A wide path led through a dark corridor in the trees ahead of Jon, a sidewalk of concrete that lead to Gaston Street and the Oglethorpe Club where he had left his van only an afternoon ago. The street was empty now. The van was gone.

He thought about Lannie the dick and wondered who would be driving #26 today.

Jon took a breath, enjoying the clean scent of the water and the open air despite the argument that had been raging for the full two hours since they left the Tunnel just before the cops arrived, and which had done nothing but escalate as Jon helped her to an all-night diner, then plied her with rot-gut coffee, sugar, and a breakfast of pancakes and maple syrup.

She had been sore, and their disheveled appearances had drawn more than the usual rash of asshole comments and judgmental stares from the night owls who frequented such places, which had done nothing but piss her off even more.

"Next time I offer to buy you breakfast," he said as he watched her pace, "remind me that maple syrup sets you off."

He had been trying the passive-aggressive approach for the past ten minutes, and it had been working about as well as the logical approach, the apologetic approach, and the let's-make-fun-of-her approach (which he knew at the time was a bad idea, but he was tired, goddammit).

Micaela growled as she whirled around and slapped both hands onto the edge of the fountain. She was an arm's reach away from him. Her hair and shoulders picked up moonlight.

"You can't expect me to kill my sister."

"She's been turned, Jon. The Dark Court controls her, and she almost killed me."

"I can't give up on her."

"That's just your stupid human side acting up."

He shook his head. "You can't bring people together with hate, Micaela. I may not be the smartest half-blood in the Harshlands, but even I've come too far to miss that lesson."

She turned and leaned on the fountain, too.

"How very kingly," she snipped.

He laughed. "Seriously. I would suck at king stuff so hard. You would be a billion times better than me."

He was shocked when she blushed.

"Yeah, well, that's not happening."

They sat without speaking.

The sound of tires on asphalt hissed in the distance. The groan of a street cleaner turned a corner.

He rotated his shoulder. In reality, he felt like he'd been given a few hundred turns in a cement mixer. He wasn't looking forward to the next couple days as his body healed, but that was all right. Things would work out, somehow.

"Is that what this is about?" he said.

"What do you mean?"

"I don't know," Jon admitted. "All I can say for sure is that you've just saved Fae Realm, and it seems to me that you should be feeling pretty damned good about that. But instead you're going off like a lunatic about my sister, who I admit is probably someone to worry about, but is some seriously weak sauce when you put her up against saving two entire civilizations."

Micaela stewed.

"What's this really about?"

"I've still got to kick the Little Asshole's butt," she said.

"Yes," Jon replied. "A princess's work is never done."

"Her work would be a lot closer to done if you had the guts to take care of your sister."

"Goddamnit, Micaela!"

Jon leapt up, took three steps, then spun on his heel and spoke in a controlled burn.

"I get that I suck, all right? I get it. I get that I crapped the goddamned bed. And I'm goddamned sorry that I couldn't skewer my sister like you're planning on doing to your brother.

"I get it.

"I get that you're pissed off.

"I get that you saved my life, and …"

He turned and gritted his teeth, then turned back to face her.

"But enough is enough. You come into my life and start telling me what the hell to do, and I'm doing my best here, right? It's my goddamned magic that closed the gate, after all, wasn't it?"

She sat there, leaning against the fountain, her arms crossed, her lips pursed, and her gaze not meeting his.

"But I still get it all, all right?

"I suck.

"But here's my question, Micaela. What the hell do you want? That's what I don't get. What are you looking for out of all this? Why do you care so fucking much that you're jumping my shit like I've ruined your entire goddamned life?"

He stopped then, realizing he was yelling, and that he was standing in front of Micaela with his finger wagging under her chin.

Jesus Christ.

What was he doing?

He stepped back and put his hands over his head, breathing a deep lungful of damp morning air and trying to get his shit back together.

He was shaking.

He turned back around, and let out a sigh of relief when he saw Micaela was still leaning against the fountain. He had half-expected her to be gone, and the fact that she was still here made him almost weep for joy.

"I'm sorry," he said. "It's been a long time since I lost it like that."

"No," she said. "You're just being fae, and I deserved it. I'm the one who's sorry."

He stepped close to her. She smelled wonderful.

"No one ever deserves to be berated like that."

"You're welcome," she said.

"You're welcome?"

"You just said I saved your life. You're welcome."

He nodded, then chuffed with a half-grin.

"So," he said. "Why are you so angry right now?"

"You were right," she said. "You're going to be the king … you're going to leave me behind. That's the way it is. I'm used to it. It's all right, though. Really, it is. Everyone leaves me behind."

"No. That's not right. I don't want to be king, and whatever happens, we're in this together."

He looked at her.

"I'm serious, Micaela. Nobody has ever done as much for me as you've done, all right?"

She looked up at him, the moonlight glimmering in her eyes making her look like something from an anime film.

"I don't believe you," she said.

He shook his head. "I want to know who you are."

She shrugged again. He liked how her shoulders moved.

"I don't know if that's such a good idea," she said. "You're in line for the throne, after all. Everyone will think you're better than me."

He noticed she hadn't moved away from him, though. She had, in fact, leaned in closer.

"There are no ways that I'm better than you," he said. "Zero."

"That's not what Fae Realm will say."

"Well, then we'll just have to teach them to think differently, won't we?"

Her smile was a simple drawing of her dark lips across her white teeth.

"Are you ever going to kiss me?" she said.

"I want to."

"Then get your ass in gear."

He waited.

She frowned.

"Are we blood relatives?" he asked.

She burst out laughing.

"Is that why you've been so weird since the river? I mean, you're kind of weird anyway, but—"

"I'm serious, Micaela. I need to know."

She looked at him, then, stunning in the moonlight.

"No," she said. "We've got too many generations between us, for even the more prudey human genealogy nuts to worry about—and to be honest the fae don't really give a shit about—"

Jon leaned down and kissed her.

Her lips were soft, her tongue firm.

He put his arms around her waist and held her close, shuddering as her hands pressed the back of his shoulders.

The fountain kicked off. The breeze picked up, and the leaves played over the woods.

They parted.

She gave a carnal grin, and her body molded against him as she pulled him back down to her.

This time, when they parted, she put a bit of space between them.

"Now," she said. "About that time you called me a chick …"

Thank you for reading "The Bridge to Fae Realm."

If you enjoyed this book, please consider returning to your favorite bookseller's site to leave a review. Word of mouth is vital to authors. Even a brief sentence or two helps.

Leave a Review!

Acknowledgments

If you follow my website, you'll know that this story grew from a much smaller kernel to become, ahem, a little larger than anticipated. I would like to thank Eric Edstrom, Chuck Heintzelman, Kelly Shire, and Brigid Collins(why does that name sound familiar?) for their highly useful commentary along the way, and extranets reader supreme Sharon Bass for both her insightful suggestions and for her super-quick turn-around at a time when I really needed it.

I would like to thank Lisa Collins, of course, for her hands-on work with the manuscript and for making only a little fun of me as the story got bigger and bigger.

I would like to thank Eliana Bodin for allowing me the use of her artwork on the cover of this book.

Finally, I would like to Thank the members of the Uncollected Anthology project: Doyle A. Dermatis, Phaedra Weldon, Annie Reed, Leah Cutter, Leslie Claire Walker, Kristine Kathryn Rush, Rebecca M. Senese, and Michelle Lang for their very gracious offer to let me write with them. Without them, Jon and Michaela would not exist. Who knows where they will end up now?

About Ron Collins

Ron Collins is a best-selling Science Fiction and Dark Fantasy author who writes across the spectrum of speculative fiction.

His short fiction has received a Writers of the Future prize and a CompuServe HOMer Award. His short story "The White Game" was nominated for the Short Mystery Fiction Society's Derringer Award. With his daughter, Brigid Collins, he edited the anthology *Face the Strange.*

He has contributed a couple hundred or so short stories to professional publications such as *Analog, Asimov's,* and several other magazines and anthologies (including several editions of the Fiction River Anthology Series). His latest science fiction series, *Stealing the Sun,* and his fantasy series *Saga of the God-Touched Mage* are available from Skyfox publishing.

He holds a degree in Mechanical Engineering, and has worked to develop avionics systems, electronics, and information technology before chucking it all to write full-time.

facebook.com/roncollinssfwriter

twitter.com/roncollins13

instagram.com/roncollinssfwriter

bookbub.com/authors/ron-collins

goodreads.com/Ron_Collins

Website: http://typosphere.com
Email: ron@typosphere.com

Join Ron's Reader List
(Get two free books!)
http://typosphere.com/newsletter

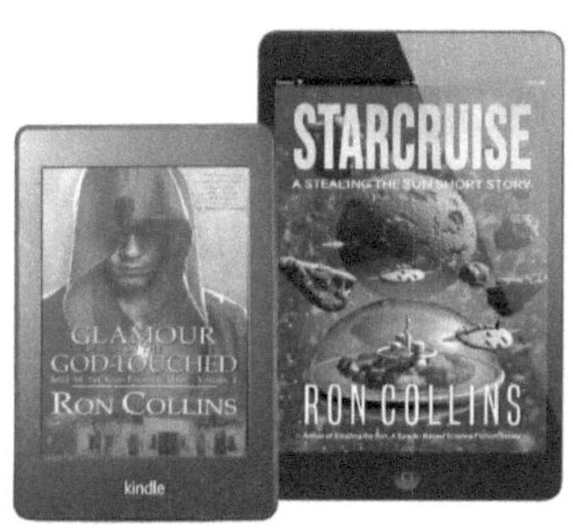

Glamour of the God-Touched
(Book 1 of *Saga of the God-Touched Mage*)

STARCRUISE
a short story in the *Stealing the Sun* universe

Also by Ron Collins

Novels

Stealing the Sun (9 books)

Saga of the God-Touched Mage (8 books)

The PEBA Diaries (2 books)

The Knight Deception

Wakers

Poetry

Five Seven Five

(Science fictional examinations of the elusive haiku)

Collections

Collins Creek (Three Volumes)

Tomorrow in All the Worlds

Picasso's Cat & Other Stories

Five Magics

Seven Days in May (with John C. Bodin)

Nonfiction

On Writing (And Reading!) Short

(A Science Fiction Writer's Quest for Stories that Matter)

www.ingramcontent.com/pod-product-compliance
Lightning Source LLC
Chambersburg PA
CBHW061458210726
48287CB00007B/2565